MW00736695

Moving Violations
A Collection of Short Stories

Nicole Amsler

DEDICATION

To Mark—who encourages me,
even though I don't write the style, POV, or genre he likes.
He knows the right words to say to keep me going.
Maybe he should be the writer.

CONTENTS

ACKNOWLEDGMENTS

The creation of this short story collection is solely due to patient friends and family who requested something—anything!—to read, to prove I was actually writing and not just wasting time on the Internet. Thank you for the nudge.

Thank you also to the vast network of stellar writers and readers who offered to critique, edit, and pummel my short stories into shape. In particular, I'd like to thank my Glitter Girls: Laurel Butler, Mary Knapp, and Kristin Shoffeitt; my Ohio muses Jeanne Estridge, Katrina Kittle, and Darren McGarvey; the kind women of BookLinks; the Cool Kids Table; the Indy Scribes, editor extraordinaire, Diana Hurwitz; and avid reader, Shaina Logemann. I am surrounded by artists who inspire me daily but particular thanks goes to Kiera Withers of Gray Barn Photography for the cover image and to Nola Cooper of Nola Cooper Designs for the cover design.

And special thanks to you, gentle reader. As much as I write for pleasure, there is a special joy in being *read*. I appreciate your time.

NICOLE AMSLER

MOVING VIOLATIONS

1

AMAZONIAN

"How are you doing, Mr. Duncan?" The neighbor lady in the Nelson's old house (Sophie? Susan?) gave me a meaningful look as she squeezed my arm.

"I'm just fine," I said, a bit too gruff as I straightened the crocheted tea towels.

"Parting with this stuff must be so hard," Sophie/Susan simpered, as she fingered the London paperweight Georgiana and I bought on our honeymoon. "Would you take $3 for this?"

My lawn held several tables of "antiques and collectibles," as the ad stated. A cherry armoire with a missing knob. A stack of afghans Georgiana knitted. Her collection of paperweights, each from a vacation or family trip. A series of delicate tea cups, elegantly painted with blooming flowers. Her unworn underthings.

"Bric-a-brac," our ever-practical daughter, Melanie had declared. "You'll feel so much freer when Momma's stuff is out of here. Your house has always been so cluttered."

"We like it that way," I groused. "It's what you get when you live together for forty years."

Melanie's modern house was decorated with iron, glass and bolts. Everything was hard and cold. There was nothing to dust, or treasure.

"Well, you could make enough money in a garage sale to travel to Australia if you got rid of this stuff. You've always wanted to go to Australia."

"No," I sighed, fingering a macramé plant hanger Melanie had tossed at me. "That was Georgie."

In the end, I had been coerced into holding a garage sale. God, how Georgie loved garage sales. Melanie was in full negotiating mode, hawking her mother's treasures to the highest bidder.

"Dad, does this humidifier work?"

"Yep. Brand new," I called over the heads of several ladies from church. They had brought casseroles over after Georgie died. In unison, they lifted their fluffy heads, smiled and batted their sparse eyelashes at me.

Rosalie, one of Georgie's bridge buddies, held up a pale pink nightgown. Georgie hadn't worn it since before Melanie was born. The filmy fabric barely covered a quarter of Rosalie's robust bosom. I suppressed a snicker. Just then, Rosalie caught my eye and waggled an eyebrow at me. I did snort then but pretended it was a sneeze from the dusty trophy I held.

"Excuse me, sir, but I don't see a price on this."

In his palm, he held out an oversized ebony and ivory brooch. Edged in silver filigree, the center was a relief carving of a regal Amazon woman. She held a spear and wore a loin cloth. Her right breast was concave while the other was firm and lush. The piece was the size of a hotel bar of soap.

Turning, I snatched the item out of his hand."This is NOT for sale!"

"I'm sorry. I didn't know," he stammered, backing away from me. He was a foot taller than my perpetually shrinking height and was dressed all in black with matching fingernails. A shank of greasy hair covered one eye while an oversized washer seemed crammed in his earlobe.

I blinked fast, holding the pin too tightly in my hand. My knuckles groaned.

"I'm sorry," I stammered, "I didn't know this was here. You see, my daughter has been helping and this is very important…to me."

Twenty years earlier, I had hovered over her hospital bed.

"What is this?" Georgiana had asked, holding the brooch in between her fingers like a dirty rag. "Oh! She's naked!"

Suddenly, I felt very stupid, the hospital lights illuminating my mistake.

"Wait, wait! You see, she is an Amazon woman. You know, those women who cut off their breasts so they could hunt better."

Reflexively, Georgiana clutched the hollow in her own chest. She flinched as she touched the new wound—or from the thoughtlessness of my gift. Covered in bandages, you couldn't see the damage but it was my hope that the sacrifice of a breast would save my wife.

"Amazon women are notoriously strong," I tried again. "Nothing could hurt them."

I had been wrong. It wasn't a significant gift. It wasn't a talisman to protect my wife. It was a tacky reminder of what she lost.

"Oh, Richard…" And Georgiana sobbed.

I reached over and patted her IV-pierced hands uselessly. Our fingers intertwined in the familiar pattern and her thumb stroked mine, a comfortable tradition we had practiced from our very first date. As her sobs slowed, I eased the pin away.

"No, don't." Her reddened eyes met mine. Determination sparkled underneath the steely blue. "Pin it on my hospital gown."

"Are you sure?"

Her shoulders straightened under the cotton gown.

"Yes, Richard," she said. "I'll be your Amazonian queen."

Still holding the pin, I watched the lanky boy back down the driveway. Tattoos ran down his arms while his pants slouched down his legs.

"No, wait!" I heard myself say. "Please?"

He looked even more startled. Melanie and the widow-watchers glanced up from across the yard as I shuffled down the drive towards him.

Warily, he had stopped, glancing at a beat-up Nissan at the end of the drive. A shadowy child-like figure was in the front seat. His fingers fluttered out towards the car, bidding "Hello" or "Wait."

"Who did you want it for?" I asked, intrigued as to the lure of a classical piece for a ruffian like this boy.

"It was for my wife," he mumbled back at me, eyes shifting to the car. He didn't look old enough to be married but my judgment was often off. I was sure my cardiologist was no more than 16.

"Do you know what this is?" I asked, already knowing his answer.

"A pin."

"No. This!" I pointed, frustrated at the relief etching. "The carving. Do you know what it is?"

"No. It's just some chick," he answered, attitude flooding his words. His black eyes—was that eyeliner?—met mine defiantly.

Still perplexed, I asked, "Why did you want this for your wife then?"

He had already started walking away, tired of our conversation.

"I don't know. Something about the girl reminded me of Phoebe, my wife." His voice lowered, almost too quiet for my failing ears. "She looked so strong."

As if on cue, Phoebe emerged from the car. She opened the creaking door and leaned heavily on it. She was frail little thing, dressed in all black including a black and white checkered scarf tied tightly on her bald head. Purple circles punctuated her grey eyes.

"Do you love her?" I asked, urgently as he quickly walked to her side, steadying her.

"Yeah." An intense protectiveness shone through as he pulled the tiny girl to him, sheltering her.

"And are you a strong woman?" I shifted my gaze to her, aware of the strange conversation she suddenly found herself in. A diamond sparkled in her nose, lost in the freckles.

"Yes." Her chin jutted out like a little girl's but her eyes were fierce. It was a look that brought tears to my own eyes.

"Then this is for you both." I stepped forward and pressed the brooch into her hand. "Wear it well."

The boy snaked his hand down her tattooed arm and knotted his fingers with hers. Her thumb randomly stroked his hand while she studied the brooch in the other.

"So who's the chick?" he asked with sincere interest.

"It's an Amazon woman," she answered, quietly. Our eyes met, knowingly. I prayed she would explain the sentiment better than I had so many years ago.

"Thank you," they said in unison. I nodded and inched back up the drive.

As the car door slammed behind me, Melanie met me at the shoe cart.

"What was that about?" she asked accusingly, glancing at my empty hands and noticing the lack of money.

I turned back to the car, as it rumbled to life. In shadows, I saw his arm slung over the seat, pulling her towards him. And I saw her clutching the brooch to her heart. With a growl, they sped away.

"They just reminded me of me and your mom."

Melanie snorted and I shot her a weary look.

"When we were young and invincible," I said. "When we fought battles and won."

MOVING VIOLATIONS

2

BAGGAGE CLAIM

Author Note: Maria Wolkefeld was a real person and the facts referenced in this story are true, however, the story itself is a work of fiction. I encourage you to read up on the Nadra Riots *after* finishing the story.

"NAME PLEASE?" THE AIRLINE CLERK ASKED, pulling my ticket and ID towards her.

"Maria Berta Wolkefeld."

It mattered naught to them that the name was false, even though the first name appeared on my Singapore birth certificate and my surname was borrowed from my stubborn Dutch husband. The name was a costume, a strait jacket.

"And the reason for your trip?" the clerk asked, bored. Her mood ring clinked on the counter with a flat thud repeatedly.

"I'm flying to the Netherlands for my mother's funeral."

"Sorry." She snapped her gum and slid the paper cards

back to me. "Put your luggage up here."

She motioned to the scuffed metal rise and I slid my Samsonite suitcase towards her. She knocked on the hard plastic case and waited, perhaps for something to answer. She thumbed my blank luggage tag while attaching a violent yellow ribbon marked Heathrow #13.

"You should really fill out your luggage tag," she said.

I didn't answer so she shrugged, sliding the luggage behind the counter. What name should I have penned? The names on my birth certificate, the ones I'd been called?

Maria?

Bertha?

Berta?

Huberdina?

Nadra?

They were all false, yet held the morsels of truth. The only truth I could claim was on a slip of paper I tore from a library encyclopedia and carried in my wallet.

The print shows a grainy picture of me and my Ibu—my adopted mother—with the printed words so black on white paper.

Maria Hertogh Riots *(or Nadra Riots) in Singapore (1950.) Maria Hertogh, a Dutch girl, was raised by Aminah Mohamed, a Muslim, for eight years. Through court decisions, she was legally returned to her Catholic parents on December 11th, 1950 at age 13. During the court proceedings, Maria married 22-year old Mansour Adbai which was nullified when she was returned to her biological parents. Subsequent riots broke out in Singapore, killing 18 and injuring 200.*

I am Maria.

I was Nadra,

I am Dutch.

I was Muslim and Malaysian.

And I was responsible for eighteen dead souls.

As I proceeded past my check-in counter, a familiar song

started behind me. Not a song but the lyrical language of Malay. I turned, hunger pangs for my home language. It was never heard in the Netherlands and seldom in London.

"Pukul berapa kapal bertolak?" The petite couple resembled brown nuts with peaked hats. They spoke with slow urgency but the girl didn't understand them at all.

"May I help?" I asked, turning to the couple, asking them to repeat themselves. *"Tolong ulang sekali lagi."*

Relief flooded their faces and they were rapid in their tale of woe, lost luggage and a missed flight. I translated between the now-helpful clerk and the lost couple.

The woman bowed, kissing my hands and thanking me, *"Terima kasih."* I smiled, embarrassed for the attention.

"Siapa nama anda?" they asked.

What name to give? Nadra was a common name but also a cursed name.

"Maria," I said.

They grinned, patted my hands again and hurried towards their concourse.

"How odd. How'd you learn that language?" the clerk asked. "You don't look Chinese."

It was not worth explaining that it wasn't Chinese but Malaysian, that I heard the language in my dreams but hadn't dared speaking in decades.

"I visited there once," I said, not a lie but a pale ghost of the truth. I walked away.

Why had I answered Maria? It was my legal name, like Huberdina, but I never used Maria except when I first began parochial school, borrowing a bit of its holiness and anonymity. It was a short lived disguise.

As if speaking an accusation, I heard Samir's voice behind me, calling the correct name, my mother's name for me.

"Berta. Over here."

He was the color of summer sand, with dark whorls of

hair on his thin arms and two caterpillar eyebrows. Since I was doing the choosing of my sexual partners now, I chose the tree limbed brown Indonesians of my childhood rather than the pale, blonde beefy men of my homeland.

I leaned in to kiss him three times, a Dutch habit.

"Not here," he hissed, pulling away. His dark eyes flashed around the bustling corridors.

I wilted like spinach. He was married (as was I) but he was far more proper in public context than I. London was his home while it was only my temporary refuge. And now I was leaving. I should be grateful that he came to say goodbye. We so seldom met in public.

I thought of my empty luggage tag. Perhaps I should have written "Philanderer." But that term was only used for men. There wasn't a proper word for philandering women. Once again, I was ill-defined. Un-nameable.

Samir cupped my elbow and guided me to a lounge in the first terminal. My macramé purse bumped passersby and I apologized over my shoulder. I was always in the wrong place. It was a curse which followed me into middle age.

It was a curse which began by being Dutch in Indonesia, by being a *Puteh* in a dark, spiced land. I shouldn't have been raised Muslim by Ibu, who should have understood I was on loan only, available to be repossessed at any time. By being Muslim, held hostage in a convent, my wrong place caused panic and death and wrote the history lesson, defining me only as "Maria, a Dutch girl."

And I certainly shouldn't have fallen in love with Mansour in those fragile days.

Samir found two seats in a quiet corner. Peering through the thick glass that shuddered with every takeoff, I could see a duplicate concourse with the same seating, ticket desks and doors. A parallel universe existed just across the tarmac, the road not taken.

"Must you leave?" Samir asked, petting my pale hand in

his own dark one. "You do not even like your mother."

This was true.

"It is her funeral. It is expected that I attend."

With embarrassment, I recalled the awkward call from Carolien, my abandoned daughter who was old enough to call the emergency number I'd left Johan, my abandoned husband. Mother's soul had slipped away in the night, leaving behind a soiled bed and a shallow indentation on the mattress. She had been disappointed that I had left once again, failing my children, my husband, my family, and her. It wasn't the first time I ran away and Mother always got her way. I was returning once more.

Perhaps I should have written "Disappointment" on my luggage tag.

I told Samir none of this and instead stole a kiss, disregarding his caution. His lips tasted of beeswax and sweet coffee.

"I could come back to London," I suggested. "If it was something you wanted to pursue."

"Berta…"

It was a pathetic conversation, one in which Samir reminded me of his impossible situation, his inability to leave his wife. He pointed out that I was not divorced

either, with ten children at home and now responsibilities in another country.

"I came to say goodbye because I knew you wouldn't return to London. Just as you didn't return to France or Greece last time. Just like you've never been back to Singapore. I've enjoyed our time together but I knew today would be goodbye."

"Do you even love me?" I asked, pitiful, so very pitiful.

He shrugged, reaching for his cigarettes and lighter. The bright tip punctuated the remainder of his lecture.

"How did you expect this to play out, Berta? That I

would leave Katherine and marry you, giving you my last name before you even dropped your previous one?"

I shifted my purse with my ankle, fearing he could read the truth on my face. My checkbook was filled with school-girl doodles of various name combinations. The potpourri of my first name options and his steady traditional surname.

"Can you lend me some coins? I need something in my stomach," I asked, avoiding the conflict. He nodded, pulling out his wallet wordlessly.

As I slid the metal disks into the machine, I calculated my worth. I was one of the few people with a price tag, my stock rising and falling on whims.

At age five, I was traded along with a sewing machine to Ibu, the practical machine sweetening the pot. Eight years later, Ibu refused the $500 my mother offered as payment for services rendered. And of course, eighteen costly souls are tabulated in my column by Mother's God.

And now I traded a declaration of love for coins.

When I returned with a Pepsi, Samir was already standing, readying himself to leave. I could be nothing but resigned.

"I should go. I probably shouldn't have come," he said.

"I understand," I said, not understanding.

Something in me was both un-nameable and broken, repulsing others. Other people had soft, pilled exteriors that attracted and kept loved ones like burrs on flannel. I was vinyl, slick and releasing.

Samir pecked my cheek and walked away, his tall frame shuffling behind crowds of people and eventually disappearing.

It was said the Maria Hertogh Riots for the western world—the Nadra Riots for the eastern—were spurred by religion. The Muslims and the Christians both felt disrespected, slighted. It was disconcerting to see a stub-nosed white girl wearing a hijab, just as it was disrespectful to see the same girl, raised as Muslim, holding the Reverend Mother's hand in a convent.

Much debate went into whether it was proper for a devout Nadra to be housed in a convent or whether a poor Maria was happy to be rescued at last from her jungle upbringing. More arguments were stirred from the exposè photos of me praying at the church's altar or leaning into the Reverend Mother. The clashing opinions resulted in eighteen dead.

But no one ever asked me.

I would have told them that I clung to the Reverend Mother's hand because she had the same soft whiskers on her cheek as my Ibu.

Love was my religion. Love for Ibu, the only mother I knew. Love for rice dumplings and rendang. Love for the fog that rolled over the village, muffling the housewive's thumping bread. Love for Mansour and the way he straightened his bent glasses with ink stained fingers.

But love was as fickle as religion.

My prayers still came like the tide, starting with *fajr* and ending with *isha*. My internal compass can always find *qiblah* for prayer. These things could not be washed away by holy water and rosary indentations in my hands. I was neither Catholic nor Muslim. And I was excommunicated from love as well, maternal and eros.

Without Samir, I wandered the aisle, eventually buying a chocolate bar and the Daily Dastak, the Netherland's newspaper. I never forgot the Malaysian language but the written Dutch language still stretched my capabilities.

I was probably the only person who never saw the original print of her wedding portrait, only owning a newsprint copy. Perhaps Mansour or Ibu had the original print. Perhaps it was destroyed, an exorcism of the Puteh, the white ghost. Be gone and good riddance, Nadra.

I could envision the photo unbidden, its pixels imprinted

on the back of my eyelids. The photo mocked me. My younger self stared back at me with heartbreaking trust. Ibu sat in the forefront, skeptical and wizened, her thin glasses tipped on her nose. Mansour was to my right, so crisp in his white suit and black cap. I remember shyly kissing those lips only twice.

I do.

And goodbye.

Only it wasn't meant to be goodbye. He promised, as did Ibu. They would fight for me, bring me back home, back to my family in Malaysia. Allah would hear our prayers. What could their Catholic God do that ours could not?

Flipping the page, I caught a familiar name in the obituaries.

Adeline Hertogh.

Mother.

She was accompanied by an older photograph, her pinched face less wrinkled but still accusing. She did not smile, but then again, she never did.

The newsprint made it real, just as print validated my child-bride marriage, proved my other mother once held me possessively in her draped arms, and corroborated the price paid for my freedom from home: death and sorrow.

Tearing my eyes from her flat face, I watched a small white vehicle, no bigger than a VW bug, push the engorged jetliner back, keeping it between painted lines. Then the small vehicle began pulling forward, dragging the mammoth plane behind. How odd that a massive entity could be so easily manipulated by a small automobile.

Returning to the page, I recalled her stark, frigid face, when I was thirteen and bandied about like a shuttlecock. In the match point, a fat man who mispronounced my name smacked his gavel down. Ibu gulped a sob. Mansour exhaled like a leaky tire. Adeline smiled. She stood to embrace me, but her lawyer held her elbow. She gave him a hard, angry look. It was a look I would become familiar with as mother attempted to exorcise Ibu's influence from my very being, replacing it with a good Dutch girl who didn't exist. Berta was a figment of mother's imagination, a ghost in the parallel concourse.

I was forced away from Ibu and Mansour. Tears blurred everything. I heard shouting, but I only sobbed. It was a 13 year old's prerogative to expect the world to revolve around her. But in my case, it had.

I returned to mother's obituary. It listed all the remaining family member, including Berta Wolkefeld, a name better buried than used.

I curled the thin paper into a tube and slid it into a cigarette receptacle. I wished for a funeral pyre but didn't see any smoldering butts.

On the plane, I settled in the corduroy seat, arranging my purse beneath my knees. It wasn't long before my seatmate arrived, a tall, willowy woman with south of Italy coloring.

"Scusi," she said, shifting past me. She looked like a Natalia or a Sophia.

She settled in and, as the stewardess demonstrated the seatbelt clicking, leaned over to speak.

"I'm terrified to fly," she said, white wine on her breath. "My name is Sophia, by the way." She extended an elegant hand. I had been right.

"Nadra," I said. "My name is Nadra."

3

DEAR CROSSING

PERCY SHUDDERED AND QUAKED when shifting from third gear to fourth, Ron noted. The company mechanic swore up and down that Percy, his truck, was pristine for the 1,300 mile journey. Ron trusted the grease monkey almost as much as he did Percy.

Fiddling with the radio, Ron put the unease he felt out of his mind and surveyed the grey stretch of road in front of him. His directions were written in a dry erase marker on the glass, just to the left of his view. He had only been on the road seven hours and already his back ached. He longed to stretch his cramped legs out across the sleeping quarters of his truck, but he was two states away from relief.

A red station wagon flew by him on the left, startling him for a moment. As they flew out of sight, he saw two kids playing in the back, unbuckled and unsafe.

Man, that irked him.

People were so foolish with their own lives. He had

passed too many bloody scenes to want to see another.

Up ahead was a Greyhound and two more trucks, including a skateboard and a bobtail. Gauging the traffic behind him, he thought "now or never" and eased over to the left lane before the next hill. He gained on the Greyhound quickly. His cab was eye to eye with the passengers, so he took a quick peek at them. Nothing out of the ordinary, bunch of people reading, a few men sleeping, a group of teenagers huddled in conversation. He slid his eyes back towards the road and accelerated slightly but just as the truck passed the half way point, a glint of red blonde hair caught Ron's eye. Holding steady, he glanced over to the Greyhound.

It was her!

It had to be.

For seven long years, Ron had fallen asleep to thoughts of that same hair draped across his shoulder. Sheila had been the love of his life but he had been too drunk to even know it.

"Baby, I can't live like this," she had pleaded, her brassy hair cascading down one side of her round face. A tiny scar marred her lip.

"Well, I don't know what to tell ya then." He had stood at the kitchen sink in their apartment, a bottle of Seagram's half gone behind him. They had had this conversation over and over again but he never thought she would actually leave. She never had before.

It was two years before an extended stay in the county jail had sobered him up. Sick of his graying face and bloodshot eyes greeting him in the mirror every morning, he had joined AA and took a long distance trucking job to stay out of bars and to give him a place to sleep.

"The open road is my home," he'd tell other truckers and the occasional friendly waitress. But home had been with Sheila.

Having slowed his truck, he could see her burnished hair. It was shorter but had the same loose curls. As if she knew he saw her, she turned profile. It was her! Her scooped nose and round cheeks were unmistakable. She even fingered a curl the same way she had over every meal and conversation they shared. The familiar but forgotten gesture made his stomach lurch and his groin warm.

She was talking to someone next to her. Who? A husband? A friend? Her mother?

She gestured mildly and smiled. She was happy.

The thought was both comforting and devastating. Ron fought the urge to wave. He considered blowing the air horn but was afraid of startling the bus driver. As it was, the driver was eyeing Ron's rig warily in the long rearview side mirror.

Ignoring the bus driver and the growing traffic behind him, Ron stared at Sheila while glancing begrudgingly at the winding, climbing road in intervals.

She had been perfect. She cooked a mean homemade chicken potpie and knitted him ridiculously colored afghans. She had paid his taxes and his tickets. She had even bailed him out of jail, holding his hand in silence as they had drove back to her apartment. He could almost smell her strawberry shampoo and taste her spearmint kisses.

If she looked over, what would he do? Could he get the Greyhound to stop? What would he say to her?

"I'm sorry for everything that went wrong. I am a changed man now. I'm sober now. Five years, two months and 12 days. I have the pins from AA. I have a job and health insurance and I pay my taxes on time.
I can take care of you now. Let me take care of you now."

He had to say these words to her. How could he get the bus to stop?

Just then, a small face peeked across Sheila's lap and looked out the window. She was a miniature of Sheila:

golden red hair, same chipmunk cheeks and scattering of freckles. The little girl who was maybe six or seven pointed out the window. Ron looked.

She had witnessed a cluster of deer standing on the left side of the road. She was enthralled. As she started to pull her head back, her eyes—his eyes—shifted to the truck. And then she was gone.

Shocked, Ron tentatively did the math in his head. If she was six...

He dug through his alcohol-soaked memories of that last night.

"I can't live like this anymore," she had said. "Not now."

As his heart reached out, the lumbering Greyhound eased to the right and exited off to I-74.

"No!" But the bus was already out of reach. Panicked, Ron considered every option.

It was crystal clear. He would find her again. He'd use the internet to look for her. He'd track down her family. He'd move heaven and earth to find her and that little girl again. He'd find her and make them a home.

He tore his eyes from the off ramp and refocused just in time to see a flood of red lights directly in front of him. Two small children, unfastened in the back of their wagon, stared up at him, their eyes wide. Without hesitation, Ron cranked the wheel hard left and felt the bottom drop out as he ran the truck down a steep embankment into a stony river below.

4

RE-HEARSED

THROUGH STINGING EYES, Tory saw only psychedelic purple. The strobe lights from the police cruiser painted the tree line blue then red, red then blue. The effect was nauseating so she placed the back of her hands against her eyes and hummed, concentrating on her breath and the vibrato. It was a typical backstage trick.

"Ma'am, are you sure you don't want to sit down?" The policeman asked, his voice breaking through her bee drone purr. He touched her shoulder and she cringed, removing her blinders.

He called her ma'am. She was 15, out for driving lessons. The darkness must disguise her age. Either that or it was her stage presence.

"No, I'm fine," she said, a blatant lie. Blood pooled in her sock. She felt the squish. It dribbled down her face as well, adding more red to the landscape. She'd be sore tomorrow, that was for sure. She might have to bow out of the Saturday matinee. But what about Rick? Would he be sore, or dead?

The policeman placed a scratchy blanket around her shoulders, then left her to slip slide down the hill to his partner. The hearse was upside down in the ravine, flipped like a coin, its wheels still, going nowhere.

The two policemen were checking on Uncle Rick, who was draped across the windshield wipers, the shattered glass a lion's mane.

Headlights appeared at the top of the hill, slowed by the strumming strobe. A practical sedan crept by. A small child and her parents peered out at her through dark windows. They stared at Tory's defiant form, alone in the road, the policemen hidden from view. What did they guess? A deer strike? A texting teen? Did they want an encore performance?

A screaming ambulance tore over the rise, prodding along the gawking family. The ambulance braked perilously close to the edge of the bend and to Tory.

The pair of EMTs flew at her, giving her a cursory assessment before sliding down the leaf strewn hill, emergency gear making the tumble with them. The two outclassed police men now started the long struggle back up the hill, arriving with their standard questions.

Prepared with her fabricated story and shocked guilt, she inched over to their car to settle her shaking knees. She was grateful for the reeking navy blanket, which smelled of car tires and tacos. It wilted behind her like an ineffective superhero cape.

The cops questioned her among the staccato lights. She answered affirmative to each of their leading questions, imagining lights as a lie detector test. Red for lie. Blue for truth. She tried to answer on blue.

"So you only have a learner's permit. Were you out practicing?"

"Yes, sir." Blue.

"Were you going above the speed limit or did something startle you? A deer maybe?"

"Actually, a rabbit." Red.

"So you swerved to avoid the bunny? And you lost control?"

The cops exchanged a loaded glance, one jotting notes. Tory exploited her long glossy hair, demurely tucking it behind her ear. It was sticky with blood. But she earned the same doe-eyed panting the high school boys gave her.

"I don't know what happened," she stammered. She twisted her fingers along her hair, a practiced nervous gesture. She pulled the hair taut all the way to her chest. The men's eyes followed her fingers like obedient puppies. Their eyes snapped back up to her face, guilty and overcompensating.

"Honey, I don't think you have to worry. It's a rookie mistake. A licensed adult was in the car with you. Your uncle should have been wearing his seatbelt but thank goodness you were."

She attempted a weak smile, rubbing at her neck where it truly did hurt from the seatbelt's violence. She finally had a telltale red mark on her neck. It felt like a coveted trophy.

"Hey, dude." One of the EMTs poked his head over the berm, seeing only the cops, not noticing her. "Guy's gone. We're gonna need a winch to pull him and the hearse up the hill."

Tory suppressed a smile.

Tory hadn't wanted her driving lessons in a hearse. Between the family business and her extracurricular activities, she was already in the limelight.

"Oh please," her mother said, never removing her eyes from the delicate stitches she was adding to Mr. Etchison's lips. "I learned to drive in a hearse and unless you want to wait until your father and I hit a lull, you need to take opportunities when they arise."

Uncle Rick, her dad's brother, had offered to take her out but his car was in the shop, again. It was the hearse or nothing.

Ever since Tory learned about Charon's obol, the coins slipped into the dead's mouth for ferry passage, she was tempted to try it. But her mother's intense scrutiny of her clientele would make the experiment short lived.

"Whatev."

Tory's mother did look up at Tory's tone of voice with pursed lips. If she yanked hard on her sewing thread, Mr. Etchison's lips would purse just like that. Instead, she yanked on the scarf at her neck. Today it was blue.

"It's nice of Uncle Rick to offer to help. Be nice and say thank you."

Tory sighed deeply, inhaling the usual scent of the cold room: formaldehyde, pancake makeup, and fresh dry cleaning.

"Be back before nightfall," her mother called out, snipping the final stitch with her favorite silver scissors. Her mother knew the location of her precious scissors every minute of the day. But some days, unless Tory sprawled out on a cold slab, her mother barely noticed her. And she didn't need any more of her father's attention.

Her mother hadn't even mentioned the electric blue eyeliner Tory wore.

When Uncle Rick strolled in the kitchen, he had his usual Citgo's Styrofoam coffee cup in his hand. He looked like Tory's dad but a squashed, stunted version. Both brothers featured a non-existent chin and a dark mat of fur on their arms and chest. Their chest hair appeared in a straight line at their neck, as if trimmed with a guillotine.

"Ready to drag race, kiddo?" he asked, taking a swig of his coffee.

"Hardly," she said, not rising to the bait. She jangled the

keys and headed to the garage which connected their home and the morgue. The black, practical hearse sat in the only parking space. Tory's bicycle hovered above it, suspended on a noose of wires along with old winter sleds and yard games she had never played as a child. She was too busy at rehearsals and productions, anything to escape her home and morgue.

"Cruising in the Caddy." Rick patted the top of the roof, which was pristine leather. Her father polished it before and after every funeral, even if there were two runs in one day.

Tory's father, Dan, married into the death business and took to it easily, attending mortuary school even before the wedding. Uncle Rick was employed by the funeral home as a handyman, a groundsman, and the occasional emergency pallbearer. Death was the family business.

At the end of the drive, Rick pointed her out of town. She dutifully stopped at every stop sign and the one traffic light. She waited for a combine to lumber by, before crossing onto 8 Mile. She chose the familiar path to the next town, Hazenville, through an alley of corn stalks and sloping hills.

"Turn left up here," he said, indicating the back access road to the dam.

"Okay," she said, slowing to make the corner.

Maybe he wanted her to practice backing into a space in the wide field overlooking the dam. They should have done that in town. She guided the hearse over the rutted drive to the edge of the grassy lawn. To the right, Penny Lake sat serenely, while to the left, water churned several stories down emptying out into the Crossley River. The dam was wide enough to drive across, but studded with concrete pillars, grates, and an abundance of fences. A concrete generator building was on the other side of the dam, its inner workings hidden from view.

"Do you want me to back up?" she asked, putting the

hearse in park then reverse.

"Nah. Go ahead and shut off the car. We'll stick around here for a minute."

She turned it off, leaving the keys in the ignition, and twisted slightly toward Rick. He stared intently at the calm waters.

"What are we doing?" Tory asked.

"Educating you."

"Yes, but what are we doing *here*?"

When Rick turned toward her, his eyes unreadable, dark, glistening, and focused.

"Do you know the interesting thing about the death business?" he asked, breaking eye contact. "I discovered this back in high school, when I dated your mother."

"I didn't know you dated Mom." Tory placed her hands at ten and two, trying to imagine Uncle Rick and Mom together. It wasn't hard. The brothers were almost carbon copies.

"Not for very long. Not when your Dad got ahold of her. But I discovered then that sex and death are closely related. They are two sides of the same coin."

He paused and Tory's eyes wandered to his crotch, which was bulging. Her throat seized and her hands slicked. A terrible sense of déjà vu flooded her, rushing over like a broken dam. If she started the car, she could back out, take them home. She could unwind the moment.

"Don't," he said, taking the keys out of the ignition. "This is part of your education. We are here to teach you a lesson."

As he spoke, he unthreaded his belt and unfastened his pants.

"You need to understand how it works in the real world. You think you need to learn how to drive and how to parallel park. You might even think you need to learn how to get out of this town. But the real life lessons you need, no one is going to teach you.

"The sins of the mother visit the daughter. And you need to learn the lesson your mother never got. You need to know how to please a man, how to bring him pleasure. It's a skill that can only be learned through experience. No book learning.

"Now open up and say ahhh."

"No. Please?" She hated how weak her voice was but she also knew before she spoke that nothing would change the next few moments. She knew how this played out.

"Now don't give me any trouble," he warned, slapping the belt across the back of her neck and unclicking her seatbelt. "Death and sex. They go together. You'll see."

It was horribly familiar. The purple protruberance from his pants, dry and chapped. The tightness of the belt around her neck, making her closed eyes swim in stars. The brutal hand at the back of her head, knotting her hair. The hot mayonnaise down her throat. The tears that wet his dark pubic hairs.

And then it was over.

She sat rod-straight in the driver's seat, swallowing repeatedly to get the taste of him out of her mouth. She knew not to puke. It would mean doing it all over again.

Like a skipping record, she knew she would be visited again and again. She studied the rushing waters through dry eyes, wondering if the force of their rage was enough to wash her clean.

Rick exited the car to refasten his pants and rethread his belt. When he reseated himself, he handed her the keys. They clicked their seatbelts in unison and he fingered her neck. The reddening was lessening and it would be as white as the dam froth by the time they reached town.

"You did good, kiddo. Let's log an hour before it gets dark, and then we can go out again next weekend."

Tory reversed the hearse and bumped along the access

road, reentering 8 Mile.

They wound along country roads in silence as the dusk settled. Rick even dozed as Tory negotiated switchbacks, passing bucolic farms and farmhouses, and three different water towers, each emblazoned with the town's name. She tracked the minutes, biding her time.

Tory even passed a deer, grazing at the side of the road, its eyes glittering and accusatory. She flew by it, unflinching.

"We should probably head back," Rick said, yawning and stretching. "Where are we?"

"Pretty far from home."

Tory tracked the road with her steady eyes, keeping watch for animals or other beasties that ambushed you from the side of the road. If only all ambushes could be identified by their telltale eyes.

As they approached the county line, she saw the hill and the bend up ahead where the dotted line transformed into double solids.

"It's time for your education," Tory said, pressing her foot firmly to the floor. "Let me tell you how it works."

Trees rushed by, the hill's angle increasing their speed to thrilling.

"Hey, hey, slow down!" Rick scrambled in his seat, righting himself from his casual slouch.

"You won't touch me again, ever. You won't touch anyone. And I don't need your life lessons. In fact, I am going to impart one to you now."

"Tory! Stop! There's a bend!"

"Sex and death," she said, reaching over with her right hand and seizing his crotch. "They go together. Two sides of the same coin."

She slid her hand away, quietly releasing his seat belt release. Then she crossed her arms over her head as they sailed into space, her foot still jammed to the floor.

Rick screamed. Tory laughed. They flew over the scrub

trees, only the fading sunset visible through the windshield. Wings clipped, they drifted low and the hearse cartwheeled down the embankment, one flip, two, three. Tory witnessed the ride through the gap between her elbows. The air bag deployed in a powdery puff, temporarily blinding her to the rest of the ride.

Ironic, Tory thought. An airbag in a car for the dead.

When they finally came to a stop at the base of the steep hill, upside down, Tory gathered her wits. The airbag was a deflated, withered thing. Rick was no longer in the seat beside her. His head and shoulders were through the front window, his body splayed on the ceiling. His seat belt was retracted neatly in its coil.

Gingerly, she released her seat belt, thumping on the ceiling. She rolled out of the hearse through the window and stumbled over broken sticks. A rabbit darted away in the distance. She picked her way around to the passenger side, rubbing at her raw neck. When she reached Rick, she knelt in the dead leaves and met his fluttering eyes. They were bloody and panicked.

"So here's your life lesson, Uncle Rick," Tory said, amused that her voice had a sexy rasp. "You should always wear your seatbelt, motherfucker."

She dug through her pants pocket and found a coin. In the hollow's dank darkness, she couldn't identify which coin it was. A nickel, she thought.

"Have you heard of Charon, the ferry man? He needs a coin, an obol to take you over to the other side."

Rick's eyes darted left and right. Tory spun the coin in her fingers. She refused to look away as his eyes blinked slower and his hands lost purchase on the shattered glass. When his breath became ragged and her pants were soaked through from the falling dew, Tory stood.

"Open up and say ahhh."

He obeyed. Perhaps to speak. Perhaps in a dying breath.

Tory teased his lips with the coin and then resolutely placed it on a pile of decomposing leaves out of his reach.

She began the long trek up the difficult hill, to flag someone for help.

The rude police lights were finally dark. Rick was carted off in another death vehicle, a dark ambulance. Tory declined calling her parents on her cell, suggesting the police just drive her home so she could prove she was okay. They had to inform them about Rick anyway. The hearse would be hauled up later and totaled out. Her dad would be pissed.

He should be grateful.

The policemen cranked the heat for her, as she sat shaking in the back seat. The EMTs had bandaged her cuts and lauded her decision to wear her seatbelt. Because of regulations, she had to take a Breathalyzer but passed.

On the drive home, the policemen kept up idle chatter.

"You are lucky to be alive, little lady," the fatter one said.

"Tell that to my dad," Tory said, still rubbing at her neck. "They will never let me get my license now."

"Accidents can happen to anyone, sweetheart. Driving at night is tricky, especially on back country roads. A hearse is probably pretty hard to handle too," he said.

Accidents could happen to anyone. But she had used this one up, unable to repeat the magic trick a second time. Tory had rehearsed the scenario in her head for so long, it seemed anticlimactic to have played out the whole scene flawlessly but with the wrong magician's assistant. The next time her father visited her room, his belt in hand, she would have a new plan.

"I'm sure your parents will just be glad you are safe. Shame about your uncle but that isn't your fault." The policeman smiled kindly at her in the rearview mirror. "You can't blame yourself."

No, she wouldn't blame herself. She would wear her

scars with pride. And she would plot a new sleight of hand, a new performance. Her education was complete. It was time to flip the coin.

NICOLE AMSLER

5

BURNT OFFERINGS

WHEN COLE ARRIVED at his estranged wife's condo to pick up Aidan, he expected a fight from Sera Ann. But she opened the door and smiled politely at him. For a moment, he wondered if she missed him, or the cabin.

"The plane tickets are purchased, the cabin is stocked, and the fish are waiting for their worms. Is the birthday boy ready?"

He kissed her, chastely, on the cheek and looked for his son, past the leftover balloons from Aidan's 7th birthday party yesterday, which Cole hadn't been invited to.

"He's been talking nonstop about it. He is especially looking forward to the peanuts on the flight," she said. "Careful!"

Aidan rounded the corner, his sturdy legs scrambling for purchase on the slick hardwood floor.

"Aw, he's tough," Cole scooped up the boy. "He wouldn't even cry if he knocked his head, would ya?"

Aidan solemnly shook his head and wriggled down. Tennis shoes tied and his Cards hat on, he was ready to go. Sera Ann smothered the boy in hugs and kisses.

"Make sure he wears both sunscreen and bug spray." She gave him a last kiss on his forehead.

Cole pried him away and shuffled him off to the truck, refusing to comment on the tears Aidan snuffled away. He was fine by the time they arrived at the short term parking lot.

Aidan silently trailed him through the airport, following too closely, stepping on Cole's heels, and tripping him up with his suitcase decorated like a John Deere tractor.

"Watch where you're stepping, boy." Cole clamped onto the boy's scrawny shoulder to guide him onto the plane. Ahead of them, a man struggled up to the counter with canes strapped to his arms. Probably a stroke. Such a waste to live a life after something like that. Better to go quick, Cole thought.

"What's wrong with that man?"

"Nothing," he said, shushing the boy. "Just a lost cause."

Aidan had his own ear phones his mother sent for the arm rest jack, tagged with a small piece of masking tape, and labeled with "Aidan M." The kid even had his own music player, plus a tablet to play games on, and a phone with a shiny, blinky screen. Seated next to the aisle, Aidan immediately ditched his expensive toys and pushed all the buttons on the arm rest instead.

Aidan jumped when the intercom broke through explaining the seat belt and exit procedures. There were only 36 passengers on the flight but they went through the rigmarole anyway.

"If cabin pressure should change, panels above your seat will open revealing oxygen masks; reach up and pull a mask towards you. Place it over your nose and mouth, and secure with the elastic band, that can be adjusted to ensure a snug fit. The plastic bag will not fully inflate, although oxygen is flowing. Secure your own mask first before helping others."

Cole sat back and watched Aidan explore his two foot space in the world. Take off widened Aidan's cornflower blue eyes but once they balanced on the air, humming along on the airwaves, Aidan returned to his explorations.

It was only a few years ago when he and Sera Ann flew out west for a vacation, while she was still pregnant. Life seemed to be divided into two eras: before Aidan and after Aidan. Sera Ann was an excellent mother, too good in fact. Her world shrank to include only the swaddled infant who quickly transformed into a toddler, and now a school boy. There was no room in her tiny world for Cole.

She didn't appreciate his world-expanding interests, especially the blonde. He didn't blame her. But he couldn't live in a tight, warped world. He needed more. She did too. She just didn't see it. Maybe a weekend without Aidan would give her some ideas. She could see a movie or go out with friends. He should have suggested it.

As soon as the light dinged off, the skeletal, aging stewardess wheeled up the aisle and eventually handed Aidan a bag of pretzels and a printed napkin, and another set for Cole.

"What to drink?"

"'Scuse me, ma'am," Cole interrupted, speaking loudly over the snarl of the engine just outside his window. "Are there any peanuts? For the boy here?"

"What?"

"Peanuts? Can he get peanuts instead of pretzels?" Cole said again, trying to hand back his cellophane bag of pretzels.

"Oh no, sir," she said, leaning in so he could hear her. She smelled like talc and stale French fries. "There are no peanuts on this flight. Too many people are allergic."

He didn't know what to say to that. It seemed ridiculous

that one person's issue could change tradition or custom. Getting through security was the same way. Some dipshit put a bomb in his shoe and now they all had to get scanned with full body X-rays. Someone couldn't have peanuts, so none of them could?

"What drink do you want, sweetheart?" the stewardess asked Aidan, who was softly kicking the drink cart with his new tennis shoe.

"Chocolate milk!"

"He'll have Sprite," Cole told her.

The boy pouted but didn't complain.

A little Mongoloid girl with thick glasses and almond shaped eyes peeked between the seats. Aidan waved to her shyly and she giggled before disappearing. She reappeared repeatedly, shoving her napkin and an assortment of tissues in between the crack, littering their feet with a steady snowfall of crumpled papers. Her parents seemed to be asleep or negligent because they didn't make a move to corral her.

"Here." Aidan handed her his ear buds, a small coil of cords in his small hand.

Cole reached out. "Don't give those to her."

The little girl snatched them first.

Aidan looked contrite but confused.

"Why not?"

"You don't just give people things, especially people like her. She'll just break them or keep them."

Just then, the girl's little fist showed through the gap once more. She had pulled off both small ear pieces and silver wire poked from the split cord. She dropped her offering on the pile of tissues. A black snake among the snow.

"Told ya, kiddo. You got what you deserved."

Cole jolted the seat in front of him with a firm kick and the mother sprang to life. She snatched away the little girl, who was batting at Aidan's nearly empty cup of Sprite.

The Down's kid began to cry. Cole checked his watch, wishing the minutes by so they could get some fishing in before dusk. His fingers itched for soil-crumbed worms and the sharp slice of fish fins. Just a few more hours.

Sera Ann had made him promise to sit Aidan near the aisle rather than the window.

"He's safe no matter where he sits," Cole had told her, trying to meter his voice. "He'll be with me."

She said he always snapped. He didn't. She just had sensitive ears. Sure, he screwed up a few times but he wasn't going to tiptoe around anyone, not even Sera Ann.

The slow girl was grasping through the crack once again. Maybe the window would distract Aidan.

"Here, let's switch," Cole said, unsnapping his seatbelt. "You sit next to the window so you can see the lake when we get there."

Aidan looked stricken.

"Oh no. Momma said no. She said to sit still, even if the light went off." He pointed, so solemn and sincere. "I promised."

"Well, I promised your Momma that we'd have a great boys' trip and sometimes that means keeping a little secret." Cole hovered, waiting for the boy to unbuckle and move but he sat, transfixed.

"Your Momma told you to obey, right?" Cole lifted an eyebrow—a practiced glare. This was his weekend, not Sera Ann's. Aidan slowly, cautiously unbuckled his seat belt and stood, holding his cup of Sprite like a treasure.

They tried to swap but Cole ended up pushing Aidan out to the aisle so they could swap. Aidan scurried back to his new window seat, still holding his cup. Cole settled into the aisle seat and searched for his seatbelt. The pile of tissues at their feet had been trailed out to the aisle, garnering a stern look from the snotty stewardess, who held up an impatient finger.

Just a minute and I'll come clean up your mess, she was saying with a single digit.

It wasn't a big deal. The girl was to blame. Give her the dirty look, Cole thought.

Cole clicked his seatbelt and reached for Aidan's soda when the plane bumped and jostled.

"Oh," Aidan said, not in alarm but in amusement. Oh.

Then the bottom fell out. Cole watched the trio of ice cubes hovering at eye level while the plane plummeted like Newton's apple. He almost pointed out the flying ice cubes to Aidan before his mind caught up with the danger of a plummeting plane.

And then the explosion threw the ice cubes out of the air and into an abyss.

A hard suitcase spewed out of an overhead compartment before the lights went out, slinging across the aisle and seats, shattering Aidan's pitching arm. His arm flapped like a surrender flag before they plunged into the darkness that followed.

He screamed for his mother, frantic, terrified.

As the darkness whirled around them, and Cole lost track of Aidan, the only thing Cole could see in the

midnight darkness was the illuminated lights that pointed to absent exit doors.

They cartwheeled through the sky, Icarus without his wings. It was hard to breathe; smoke and fuel smacked him in the face through the broken teeth of the plane. The sound was deafening. And then there was nothing.

When Cole awoke, it was on an alien planet. The terrain was covered in tiny, fiery trees. The sky was orange and strange. And behind his head a monster growled.

Cole tried to move and found his limbs worked in jags of pain. His lungs were filled with lava. Aidan wasn't in the seat connected to his. Smoke made day night while acid ate away at Cole's lungs and nostrils as he tried to unbuckle. The buckle was hot. It was then that Cole noticed he was burning.

In movies, burning men ran and flailed, encouraging the flames to devour them. In instructional videos, the burning man flung himself to the ground. Stop, drop and roll. Then they popped up, unscathed like a Whack-a-Mole.

In this hell, neither option was available. Cole couldn't run. His arms and legs worked on a time delay, slow and molasses-like. He couldn't drop and roll. The ground was on fire. He could only burn.

He didn't feel it. Not then. He used his sizzling eyes to search for Aidan, who he found only steps, and eons, away in a crumpled heap. At first, Cole thought it was burning laundry, but the Cards hat called out to him in the orange hell. He knelt and lifted the boy into his arms. They were chest to chest and their shirts fused together with a crunch, but it smothered the flames. Cole couldn't do anything about the rest of the fire licking at them. The boy's Cards hat melted down his neck.

"Momma," the boy whimpered.

"Shh." Cole managed, his breath expelling like a dragon.

"I'm sorry I unbuckled," Aidan said, moaning a deep, adult groan. "I'm sorry."

Cole carried Aidan, who continued to moan, the feral sound of a trapped cat. He didn't know to where, but he walked. The monster behind him was an engine that still spun, its blades like a food processor. Cole turned away from churning blades toward the sunset sky. He didn't notice any other people or any of the wreckage. He didn't notice flames fusing Aidan's arms to his neck. He didn't notice his shoes melting away in the fiery landscape, leaving him to walk through the embers with soleless shoes which smoked from the crisp edges.

Hell wasn't underground, manned by Lucifer. It was a cornfield in Michigan, where Delta-cremated ashes danced in between corn stalks.

He would have walked all the way back to Ohio if he hadn't stumbled out of a ditch and onto a pebble paved road where he was nearly hit by a screaming fire truck.

He hadn't noticed its siren either. And then he didn't notice anything for a very long time.

***

He never woke up, not fully. The nightmare continued, hellfire flames licking his feet and climbing up his hairless legs. He woke himself, kicking the sheets, snapping taut scar tissue like bubblegum pops. Deep breaths were impossible to take in, half of his lungs were filled with inches of ash, soot, and jet fuel.

The nurses stealthily pumped narcotics into his IV before they walked brazenly back in 30 minutes later to peel him off the white sheets, like Aidan's fruit leathers off cellophane. He couldn't scream with his mouth gagged with breathing tubes. He could only gargle up jet fuel, retch it into this mouth, his taste buds and pain receptors the only functional parts of his body.

In his twilight sleep, he tried to forget everything. And for awhile he did. Black waves of nothingness carried him away only to crash him back onto shore, where his nerve endings flamed and screamed.

When it was safe enough for Cole to have visitors, Sera Ann was there with her dead, suspicious eyes.

"Aidan's gone."

He knew. This was the dark nightmare he woke to, in addition to the pain.

He had a tube jammed down his throat so he couldn't answer her relentless questions. He was grateful for the purchase of time. Still, she peppered the air with a barrage of unanswered questions.

Was Aidan scared?

Where were you in the plane?

Was he wearing his seatbelt?

Was he alive when you crashed?

Did he call for me?

Sera Ann had choked on that question, as if the answer would change the end result.

He blinked, sucking on the respirator. She came to relive Aidan's last minutes, minutes she had missed. She hadn't come for Cole. She had come to extract shards of truth from his charred body. Finally, blessedly, the thick and vicious drugs carried him away from Sera Ann's accusing eyes.

Weeks passed in a series of consecutive nightmares. He had been transferred to the Cincinnati burn unit and had just undergone another surgery on his shoulders when Sera Ann returned.

"Your shoulders took the worst of it," a nurse told him. "Your son's arms cooked into your shoulders, fusing them. We had to cut it all away, skin, meat, charred bits."

Cole remembered picking up the boy. He couldn't stop himself imagining what it looked like when they peeled him away. Is this what it felt like when they cut open Sera Ann and forcibly pulled out a blue baby, swaddled in fat pulsing cord? Could she feel phantom movements from their boy, like he could?

As he lay on the special bed which placed him face-first, aimed toward the floor, Sera Ann entered. He heard her gasp first. There was no covering on his back except for the shiny grease they added every day.

Several long minutes passed before she took a chair next to him and began her questions anew. He had no escape this time. He was grateful he couldn't look her in the eyes.

"Aidan didn't suffer," he told her in a raspy whisper, no longer the fire-breathing dragon. He told her a bedtime story version of the crash, killing their son midair by a quick blow to the head, saving him from the suffering 10,000 feet below.

She pressed for details and he provided small, innocuous ones. The creaking and groaning of the plane, how the windows popped like bubble wrap. How Aidan had enjoyed the peanuts. He told her he couldn't tell her anymore because it was too painful to remember.

It was a lie. She didn't need to know what it was really like in that bucking plane. No one needed to live through that. He couldn't bring back their boy. He couldn't unbury the coffin. But he could shield her from the horrors that visited him every night. Wasn't that what husbands were supposed to do?

"Are you sure Aidan didn't say anything? Call out?" she asked, her voice wavering in emotion.

"No, he was unconscious within seconds of the explosion," Cole said. He couldn't see Sera Ann to know if she believed him.

From his horizontal, downward facing position, he could see a section of her knee cap just beyond his shoulder. Cole once had a tattoo on his outer shoulder, high on his biceps. It was gone now, replaced with skin that swirled like frosting.

Where was it now?

It had been a handsome tiger lily, blazing orange with spotted freckles. And underneath, on a sunny yellow banner, two words, his world: Sera Ann.

The tattoo was gone now.

"Tell me about his funeral," Cole asked. What else did they have to talk about?

Sera Ann gulped a sob.

"It was a closed casket," she said, bitter.

In the hospital, they told him 60% of his body had been burnt, which translated into a 40% chance of survival. A visiting pastor who prayed with him also reported that 50% of married couples who lost a child ended up divorcing.

So how did the math work out for him? He had a losing hand.

"It should have been you."Sera Ann said the words in a hushed tone. He didn't disagree. There was nothing he could do but fold.

Cole never saw the wounds on his back. His neck didn't twist that far anymore and he didn't need to see the scars to understand the pain. He imagined them as two angry red wounds, twin reminders that he lost both his wife and his son that day. Death certificates and divorce papers would follow later.

As Cole faced the linoleum floor, studying the fissures between the black and white tiles, he grabbed ahold of the words the nurse shared with him before his surgery.

Cauterization promotes healing.

God, he hoped so.

***

On the second anniversary of the crash, Cole burnt his bagel at breakfast, the smell forcing him to retch in the sink. He rinsed away the bile and dampened a cloth to hold to his deformed nose and mouth. It reeked of sourness but it was a welcome stench over the burning bread.

It had been awhile since he had burned something. He should have been pleased. Cole threw both halves in a plastic bag and cinched it shut.

He used the advertising section of the newspaper to fan the air, experimentally sniffing it. All clear. The panic receded. This was progress he could mention to his therapist later that day, if he went.

He poured a bowl of cinnamon Life cereal instead and spooned it into his lopsided mouth. The cereal tasted like ashes. He'd have to drink a protein shake to replace the peanut butter protein he had planned to slather on the bagel.

The kitchen was too quiet. His spoon thunked into the plastic bowl. The digital clock ticked off minutes in silence. The phone sat mute, under a sheen of dust. Cole tapped his foot loudly and chewed with his mouth open to fill the space.

Slurping the milk from the bowl, he gargled with it to clear his palette. Instead he tasted burnt milk. He wrestled down another retch. He stood, cringing as his side pulled. He took a minute to breath air into his half lungs before he shuffled to the sink and rinsed the bowl.

The hours stretched out before him like an airport runway. He had hope for the afternoon, but the tasks of errand day would often wear him out for days. He had to stay strong until 3 o'clock.

***

The red and white pole spun in a mesmerizing twist. Cole sat in his parked car, listening to the two sports guys argue on the radio. His feet were getting too hot so he flipped the heat off, only to plunge into coldness. He had no temperature regulation.

Russ flipped on the blinking "Open" sign and waved at him through the lettered window. Cole tipped his head in acknowledgement but didn't move toward the door. He waited through two commercial breaks before shutting off the car and trundling into the barber shop.

"Morning, Russ," Cole said, shrugging off his coat and straining to set it on the eye-level hook. Pain raked up his ribs, as if his arms were webbed to his sides. He took a minute to catch his breath before he turned to face the barber, knowing the strain colored his ruined face.

"How you doing, Cole?" Russ asked, pity in his eyes. Pity stung like skin grafts, evoking the chemical stench of bleach and that horrible ripping pain. He preferred disgust over pity.

Russ could shrug his barber coat on and off all day long without even thinking of it.

"Fine," Cole said.

Fine.

Cole eased himself into the leather seat and shifted in discomfort. Russ draped a black cloth over his shoulders and the heft of it pressed against scar tissue. Cole concentrated on breathing regularly, watching himself in the mirror, once again startled by the monster in the mirror.

Russ stood behind him, like a guardian angel in white.

"What can I do for you today?"

The answer was always the same. Other than the eleven months of hospitalization after the accident, Cole had been coming to Russ since they graduated from high school, years ago. Russ had borrowed his cherry picker once and a set of metric socket wrenches. Yet now, with his new face, Russ treated him as if he was a new entity, a stranger.

"Just a trim. Clean up around the ears," Cole said, hating that his hair grew so fast, placed on his scalp in mottled patches like diseased grass. Each touch was a challenge not to cringe.

"Alrighty then," Russ said, pulling a comb and a pair of gleaming scissors from an ocean blue jar of disinfectant. "Did you catch the game last night?"

The comb raked over his dappled head, catching on the ridged scar at the base of his skull. Cole hoped the tight and low haircut disguised the unevenness of his remaining hair but he knew it was a fantasy. No one looked at his hair when they had to look at his face.

Russ gave his running commentary on the baseball season, favoring the Cards. Cole was only obligated to grunt or nod. When Russ pulled down on the edge of the Velcro collar, Cole closed his eyes, willing himself to stay still. Russ said nothing about the swirled scars at his neck which stretched up his face, like a finger painting gone wrong.

"I'm hoping to get to a game next weekend, with the boys," Russ said, reaching for the clippers.

Cole almost told Russ about the little league game his son had played, the one where Aidan caught the pop fly. The team wore Cardinal caps, even though they were sponsored by a heating and air company. Cole could remember the shock on Aidan's face when the ball landed in his glove. Sera Ann was so proud. Hell, so was he. They had clapped and cheered, making fools of themselves over the pile of celebrating six-year-olds. Aidan was thrilled with the catch but a juice box and fruit snack were still the highlight of playing baseball.

He might have mentioned today was the two year anniversary of the crash, of Aidan's death.

Cole opened his mouth to speak, but Russ moved onto college football, filling the air with a babble of words, creating a wall of monologue. This conversation was as holey as cheesecloth, the absent words and intent gaping like black holes.

"Need a shave?" Russ asked, using the soft bristle brush to swipe at Cole's neck and shoulders. Cole stared into his own uneven lidded eyes in the mirror, refusing to wince. He was too cowardly to ask Russ to stop.

"Nah, no shave," Cole said, finally shrugging away from the brush.

"You got something special you're doing today?" Russ asked, pulling off the collar which was both a relief and a smarting pain. Russ softly patted his shoulder and Cole couldn't repress a shudder.

"Nothing much. Just some errands."

"Well, you have a good day then," Russ said, waving away his money. Cole left a ten on the desk anyway, refusing to meet Russ' eyes as he left.

***

The rare full-service gas station was 14 miles past his

house, in the wrong direction from his other errands. He passed nine other gas stations, all with lower prices than the Sunoco on the corner of 8th and Main. But this one had full service, an indispensable indulgence.

He pulled in, driving over the cord which dinged shrilly. It was before lunch and the streets weren't crowded with the lunch time crowds of the downtown workers. He shut off the engine and stood on wobbly knees once again.

"How are you?" the Hispanic boy with the floppy hair asked.

"Fine."

Fine.

"Fill 'er up?"

"Yep, just regular grade. Probably 10 or 11 gallons," Cole instructed, limping off to the crumbling cinderblock building.

The boy would fill his tank and in a bit, Cole would step inside to pay. But first, he hid behind the building where two chipped doors flanked each side, his and her restrooms. Normally, he stood in between the two doors hidden from the gas pump and the street traffic, staring out into the scrubby back lot, counting the minutes until it was over. Restrooms were never safe to enter. They often smelled like smoke or bleach.

But gas fumes were a fist to the gut. He couldn't bear them. When he moved back home, out of rehab, he had immediately replaced his natural gas stove with a flat top electric stove. He had gotten the house in the divorce because Sera Ann couldn't keep up with the yard and acreage. Truth be told, he couldn't either. He couldn't mow the lawn or fill up the lawn mower with gas.

The smell of gas—sulphuric, sinister, and stale—could unknot the ropes in his core and he'd fall apart like a dismantled marionette doll.

Today, the tiny leftover hairs on his neck were bothering

him, activating his crazy quilt of nerve endings with incessant irritation. He was going to pop into the bathroom to rinse off his neck but the handle wouldn't budge.

He tried knocking.

Then for the first time, he noticed the sign that said, "See the attendant for the bathroom key."

A flush of blood rippled through his scars. He felt tricked. He had feigned a bathroom trip every visit for months now. What did they think he did back here without a key? Why hadn't they ever said anything? In his anger, he still trained tender fingers to his neck, attempting to brush away the miniscule irritants. So much irritated him these days.

He stomped into the store, banging the door too hard.

"How much do I owe you?" Cole asked, pulling his wallet from his front pocket. His arm didn't reach all the way around the back anymore.

"It came to $22 and change. $22 is fine though," the older Hispanic man said, not looking up. Some people could look at him. Others couldn't. Cole preferred the latter.

"No," Cole said, seeing the pity reflected at the scuffed counter. "Twenty-two and what exactly? I insist."

Cole handed the man a twenty and a five with his good hand. Once Cole saw the man smack open two coin rolls, he was sorry he insisted on exact change. Luckily he had two singles to hand the younger boy. It would have been embarrassing to ask for change.

Walking out the ringing door, he saw the younger boy twisting off the cap on a late model Buick. The owner of the car passed Cole in the door way, jostling his shoulder. Cole smothered a cry of pain.

"Scuse me," the man said.

The boy had the nozzle in his hand already. Cole could see the fume pervert the air before the scent hit him, igniting a bile-fueled fire in his belly. He skipped the tip and dove for his car. Slamming the door quickly behind him, gasoline fumes were now trapped in the car with him. He gagged three times in quick procession.

Cole jutted forward, straining the new skin on his hips and ribs, to bury his nose in the cheap pinecone paper sachet that hung from his rear view mirror. He didn't care if they could see him. He snorted in the fake evergreen scent—more perfume than greenery. The gas smell dissipated as did the mutiny in his stomach.

In a moment, he had the strength to turn the key. The nausea felt like a lingering flu. His neck itched but he couldn't scratch. And his head swam, too many stimulants in too short of a time. He just wanted to go home, crack a beer and turn on the History Channel. But he still had more errands today before returning to his tomb called home. He had to go to the graveyard.

***

The airline paid for the therapist. It was part of their compensation package. Lawsuits were filed by the four other living and families of all the dead. Sera Ann was involved in three different lawsuits and he didn't blame her.

But he hadn't filed even one. He took advantage of the therapist though because he had a problem.

Sera Ann.

Dr. Ashton couldn't tell Cole if Sera Ann took advantage of the services.

"The better use of our time would be to concentrate on you," he said, diverting Cole away from Sera Ann's mental stability. "You are the one who survived the plane crash. You witnessed horrific things. Post traumatic stress is a real issue."

Dr. Ashton didn't understand. But he'd tell Cole that it was just the PTSD talking if he blew up at him. Some days Cole just wanted to yell and shriek at the doctor, "You don't understand! The crash is over, there is nothing I can do to change it and fix it. Aidan is gone, dead. But I still have a wife, an ex-wife; one who acts like I'm dead too. Help me fix that. That is what I want fixed."

"What would you want to say to her if she was still talking to you?" Dr. Ashton asked.

Cole thought about it.

"I'd want to ask her questions."

"Such as?"

Random heated prickles peppered his side and neck. It was like getting shot with buck shot. These pains attacked without provocation and it usually caused Cole to gasp and struggle back to a normal breathing pattern.

Dr. Ashton must have decided the question hit a nerve because he leaned forward, eagerly. Cole was the nut to crack and the good doctor was the nutcracker.

Words didn't float into Cole's head but rather images with gaping black spots, melting away like film when left in a projector too long.

Cole imagined the road the fire truck found him on, and then as if a bird took flight, he rose above the wreckage, examining imaginary escape routes. Should he have walked north or west? Should he have zigged when he zagged? Could have gotten to help sooner, allowing Aidan to live, to breathe?

Cole pictured his body crumpled on the graveled pavement, his son fused to his body. Did they peel him away? Was he alive then? What comfort did they offer him?

In his mind, he zoomed to the hospital, where lights flashed by and buzzers rang. He didn't know what he retained in memory or if he was just creating a world in his imagination.

Who called Sera Ann? How did they tell her there had been an accident? Did she know immediately how bad it was? How did she get to the hospital? How did he get to the hospital?

Who spoke at the funeral? Who helped her pick a casket? How many people attended? What was he dressed in?

Cole had so many questions he was unable to ask. She held the pearls of information he needed, but he couldn't excise the flesh and cause her the pain, in order to get it. Just as he couldn't cause her pain by telling her the truth.

But in order to share, in order to swap their tidbits of story, he would have to hurt her again. And the world already had too much hurt.

Too much hurt.

Cole answered Dr. Ashton with a barrage of questions, the same ones he asked himself.

"Why do you need to know so much about what happened when you were unconscious?" Dr. Ashton asked.

"Because it's the pieces of the puzzles I still don't have."

"Don't you feel that Sera Ann feels the same way? That you have information she needs?"

Cole stubbornly shook his head. The information he had to share would only hurt. No good could come of it. Both sets of information, his knowledge and hers, would pain her.

And for that reason alone, there would be no transaction, no tit for tat, no information shared.

Dr. Ashton took another approach. He sat back, steepling his hands in front of his puffy lips. He sucked on the inside of his cheeks.

"Let's approach this from another angle," he said. "I want you to ask a question of yourself. What do you need to know from yourself?"

Cole nearly snorted. What a crock. He didn't have a question for himself.

He had questions for Sera Ann, who wasn't talking to him.

Hell, he even had some pretty rough questions for God,

who wasn't much use either.

But there wasn't much he wanted to know from himself. He could barely stand to live inside his skin, his mottled, swirled, marbled skin.

"Fine," Cole said, spitting the words. "I'll play. I'd ask myself why did you need to go on a fucking fishing trip in the first place? Why couldn't you have taken Aidan to Chuck E Cheese instead? Why couldn't you have sat in his seat? Why couldn't you have ran faster when you carried him to the road? Why?"

His questions were choked off with a sob. He was furious that the shrink succeeded, drawing up poison from his snake bite. But he was furious with himself more for breaking the façade.

How are you? Everyone asked. It was a greeting, not a question.

Fine was the only acceptable answer.

Cole used his mottled hand to swipe at tears. Two flaws, visible.

"How are you feeling?" The doctor asked, passing him a generic box of tissues.

"Fine."

***

He arrived at the graveyard at 2:20 pm, in order to park and travel to his son's graveside. There was a hill behind the modest white granite stone and a patch of trees at the top of the hill. Cole stood in the copse, hidden from view but still able to see Aidan's grave.

Sera Ann would come at 3 o'clock, as she did every week, at the hour of her son's death. On his anniversary, he had no doubt she would be punctual, bearing a Cards cap and perhaps a teddy bear.

Coles' stomach tightened in anticipation. He would only watch her on anniversaries—the anniversary of Aidan's death, Aidan's birthday, their wedding anniversary. He savored these rare moments out like a treasured Morel mushroom, stumbled upon in the dark woods.

He had nothing to say to the cold stone, glistening below, emblazoned with the name they chose from a book while Sera Ann labored. He had burnt through his apologies, his pleas, his pain and grief, cooling his scarred, tear-stained cheeks on the boy's name. But no forgiveness came. For a millennium, his son's bones would soften, crumble and be devoured by the earth that reached up to grab him from the sky.

And Cole would remain in hell.

A car door slam echoed through the studded graveyard. Cole positioned himself behind the widest tree with the best view. Sera Ann walked into view, dressed in jeans and a flowing shirt. She looked good. Cole's arms wanted to reach for her.

She walked purposefully to the grave and knelt to rest on her hip.

"Hey sweetheart," she said.

Cole's heart lurched. For a blissful moment, he believed she spoke to him, her watching husband.

She continued, placing the ball cap on the grave and telling the boy about his neighborhood friends and how the Cards were doing in the tournament. She spoke with such peace and calmness that Cole almost didn't notice the tears streaming down her cheeks. It was only in her last few sentences that her voice wobbled, betraying her emotion.

She didn't need to be alone. He could be with her. They could be a family again, even without Aidan. They could even try again. They weren't young but it wasn't out of the realm of possibility. Every bit of fused determination to avoid Sera Ann melted away. They didn't have to suffer alone.

Cole stepped out of the shadows and almost called out her name when he heard the crunch of gravel. A man walked up the path Sera Ann had used. Cole stepped back and watched, worried and cautious.

Sera Ann turned to the man and held out a hand. He walked to her and took it, kneeling beside her.

"Aidan, honey, I want you to meet Allen."

"Hey buddy."

Sera Ann smiled through her tears, stroking the gravestone she picked alone and told Aidan all about Allen and how they met. Allen sat comfortably, one hand on the grave and one hand on Sera Ann's hip. He looked at ease and even spoke to the grave a few times, adding details and laughing at inside jokes.

Cole's heart burned within him, as painfully as it had during the crash. Waves of horrible burning overtook him as he slid down the tree, letting the rough bark abuse his tender skin. He watered his flaming heart with a stream of hot, wet tears. But the blaze could not be quenched.

Many minutes later, well after the car doors slammed and the couple left, Cole struggled to his feet, crawling across the ground to an accessible gravestone and used the VanNess family's gravestone to climb up.

"Thank you," he said, genuinely grateful for the help. And he left, without saying goodbye.

***

He considered just driving home but he'd still have to cook dinner. It was just easier to eat in town. An unlabeled minivan was in the handicap spot in front of A Bonnie Café, affectionately called ABCs. It served home-style food, but it was new, which meant it smelled like drywall instead of old smoke. Cole parked on the other side of the street and walked slowly across, his graveyard calisthenics already felt in his knees.

"Afternoon. Have a seat anywhere you want. Menus are on the table."

He chose a seat in the corner, where the light was dim.

He put his best side facing the edge, where the waitress would stand. He tucked his scarred hand in his lap and read the menu.

Fish.

Why had they flown hundreds of miles away to go fishing? He could have bought fish in Dayton. Hell, he could have taken Aidan to the fish pond just down the road.

Chocolate milk.

Aidan had asked for two things: peanuts and chocolate milk. He was denied both then killed. Even murderers got a last supper of their choosing.

Cole almost stood to leave but the waitress appeared at his table, a cup of water and a coffee pot in her hand. Her name tag read "Laurie" even though her tattoo listed another name. Mirabelle.

"Coffee, hon?"

He nodded, blinking fast, trying to regain composure before she asked for his order.

"How are you today?" Laurie asked.

Fine.

She tipped her head, like she heard a whistle in the distance. Her bangs were pulled back, leaving two curtains of hair on either side. It was as if she were measuring his words, weighing them to determine if he was telling the truth.

"What can I get you today?" she asked, deciding to accept his Fine diagnosis.

"What do you recommend?" he asked, not opening the menu. He wanted to hurry the conversation, afraid she would ask what happened. She seemed like that kind of person. Women were dangerous that way. Their personal space bled into yours.

"You a meat eater?" she asked. How odd of her to ask. No, he could conjure the taste of his own cooked flesh in his mouth, his barbequed lips, grilled meat. He chose every other kind of protein but he couldn't stomach meat. He shook his head.

"The Cobb salad without the ham is my favorite. We got good quiche too, with spinach. I'll let you think on it."

She reached a tattooed arm out and squeezed his forearm. Then she was gone.

He sat, feeling electrocuted.

Why had she done that? She had squeezed the bare part of his left arm, where his real skin still existed. It didn't hurt but rather shocked. It had been so long since someone touched him, other than brisk surgeons and efficient nurses with their Brillo pad brushes.

He replayed the scene in his head. She stood, he shifted his eyes and then her hand reached out and squeezed his arm. He tried to recreate the feeling of the squeeze, the pressure, the temperature. Her hand had been warm, radiating kindness or pity. He wasn't sure which.

When Laurie returned, she was already carrying the Cobb salad without ham. She placed it down and smiled at him. He tried to meet her eyes, to thank her for the food, for the smile. Instead his eyes drifted to her arm.

"Mirabelle." He said the name out loud. Internally, he absorbed the butterflies, the curlicues, the jagged thorns.

"Mirabelle's my angel baby," Laurie said. "I tattooed her name so I wouldn't forget." She paused a bit again before carrying off another plate, a flying saucer through the air, supported by a hand beneath it.

Forget. How could a mother forget? They never did. Their blood and bones walked outside their body in the capsule of their child. Aidan was not his own. He was legacy. He was immortality.

He was a burnt offering.

Cole forced down the salad and even ordered a piece of cherry pie, mostly to see Laurie's tattoo again. He worked up the courage to ask her about it when she delivered the pie. He was out of practice talking to people besides his therapist.

"How long ago did you lose Mirabelle?" he asked, thinking of the question he wished someone asked him.

"She passed three Christmases ago, December 21st to be exact," Laurie answered, seeming happy to answer. "She was four years old."

Cole nodded. He wondered if he should say more, having opened the wound.

"I'm sorry for your loss. I just lost my son two years ago. Today."

He worried it made it seemed like he was comparing losses, as if they were transactions, as if her young daughter trumped his slightly older boy, as if Aidan's horrific death put to shame her daughter's illness.

She nodded at him, no need to share details about loss. Words could not contain the breadth and depth of grief. This was someone who knew the horrors of loss.

"Can I ask you a question?" Cole asked.

She nodded, leaning heavily on the table, waiting for the question. He was tempted to invite her to sit but he wasn't sure he could commit to such intimacy.

"What made you decide to get the tattoo of Mirabelle's name?"

He missed hearing Aidan's name out loud. His missed the boy's voice. And his laugh. He blinked back tears.

"I always knew I would," she said, easily as if he asked her about the weather. "Mira was sick for so long, pretty much since birth. She wasn't like my other kids, all fat and rosy. She was half gone as soon as she arrived."

Cole wondered if it would hurt less if he'd known Aidan would die young. Would he have held on more loosely?

"I just wanted some real pain. You understand?" she continued. He must have looked confused, because she continued.

"The pain in here," she tapped her name badged chest, "was terrible. But it was impossible to pin down. Like a leech that slipped out of my grip every time I tried to put my finger on it, to pin it in place. I needed pain I could feel. Pain I chose."

"It seems like you have seen some pain," she said, placing her callused hands on his tender one. If it hurt, he didn't mind.

"Burns are a special kind of pain," he said, repeating what his doctors told him. "It's the gift that keeps giving. Burn pain never stops, it just migrates, comes and goes."

"Yes, but nothing can burn eternally. I'm sure you have faced worse pain and came through the other side. Your burns are external badges for what you've experienced. You wear your scars on the outside, while some of us have to have ours added aftermarket."

She winked at him and stood to leave, placing a few more napkins on the table.

"You can choose pain. But you can choose to let it go too."

***

Cole feared the tattoo parlor would smell like smoke but it smelled like a hospital instead. Neither smell was pleasant. A petite girl with a series of red and black tattoos greeted him along with the door chime. Her bangs were cut high up on her forehead and she had three small studs in her forehead.

"May I help you?"

Cole didn't know if he was supposed to have an appointment. He floundered for words, but she was kind and gentle like many of his nurses. She walked him through the process and policies, assuring him that everything was sterile and safe.

It occurred to him that for once he wasn't the oddest looking person in the room. True, his scars weren't meant for beauty but her markings drew more attention purposefully. She sat on the velvet couch with him, perusing the tattoo books, suggesting inspirational artwork since he didn't know what art he wanted.

"I had a tattoo once but it burned away." He grasped his shoulder which was mottled with damaged skin, evidence of the tight pressure garments he used to wear. Everything that touched him left its mark. Aidan most of all.

"I want something to honor my son who died in a fire."

Audra, the girl, didn't say anything which was a nice change of pace. She just waited.

"I'm considering tattooing his name or his face," Cole said.

"Oh no," she said, truly alarmed. "You already know his name. And faces never turn out well, especially on someone your age, or on scar tissue which is already tricky to ink."

Cole's heart deflated. This was a stupid idea. What would Sera Ann say? He couldn't steal her son's name or face to add to his own body without permission. He had already stolen so much.

Audra gently took his arm. "Cole." She waited until he met her eyes. "This is a very important tattoo. It's not a memento or evidence. It's your memory and a tribute. You want to find an image that speaks to you. One that says more than a word or a name could. So let's try something."

She spun to nearly face him, her knee resting against his.

"Close your eyes," she said, seeing the doubt in his eyes. He obliged.

"Think about your son. Remember everything you can about him. Think about how he smelled. What his hugs felt like. Remember what he did to make you laugh."

She paused while Cole's mind was overwhelmed. He hadn't given himself permission to think about Aidan since the accident, not really. Running away from the memories had done nothing but give them legs and endurance. He embraced the flashes of happy memories and crumbled.

The tears coursed down his ruined cheeks as he brought to mind the lost boy and his uniqueness.

The way the boy always hitched his pants up when running out to the ball field.

The curl of hair over his ears when Sera Ann was late to the barber.

The studious way he pinched his ballpark peanuts, trying to crush them in his small fingers.

How the boy fell asleep under the crook of his arm when they drove in Cole's truck.

Audra still clasped his wrist and she felt like a tether to him as he struggled to regain control.

"Good. Now think of one image, just one that makes you think of him in a happy way. Think of one thing."

The image appeared in his mind like a mirage. A peanut, its slight curve and dimpled texture, its treasure found inside, was one small thing Aidan loved and was denied.

The small pen drawing made Cole smile. Cole could imagine Aidan laughing at the funny tattoo with a sense of pride in his daddy. It was the first time Cole imagined Aidan beyond his last days. If he were there, he'd laugh.

"I'd like to get two tattoos. The peanut here." he pointed to his heart where Aidan's heart had hammered against his own through a thin layer of blood, bone, and flame. "And a re-rendering of a tattoo I used to have." Complete with Sera Ann's name.

Feeling a sudden purpose, Cole easily removed his shirt and Audra began to probe his scar tissue. It was decidedly intimate.

She prodded fingers across the mottled surface, kneading it with her fingers. She explained that she had to assess the quality and depth of the skin in order to properly add the tattoo. Cole felt the usual terrible pain but didn't flinch away from it. He chose this pain and it would end soon.

Long minutes passed while she smoothed, massaged, and poked his chest and arm.

"How are you?" Audra asked.

"Ready. Worried. Excited." It was the first time he hadn't lied. He was not fine and he refused to offer up the false word in community conjecture anymore. From now on, he would offer an honest answer.

As the tattoo machine began to buzz and the first bite of flesh was colored with blood red ink, he finally felt just fine.

6

BEAUTY AND THE BEAST

THE IDEA OF GOING TO O'HARE airport in my red negligee to protest the TSA's overzealous searches sounded clever two days ago, after four Mojitos, and surrounded by my sorority sisters.

"If the TSA want to strip search us on our way to Spring Break, we'll save them the trouble!" Bree had declared to the throng in our common room.

But standing alone in front of the swooshing doors, I only felt alone. The cab ride had been awkward to say the least.

I ignored the catcalls and pounded out a text to Bree. "Where are you?"

"On board. Gone in five. Where are YOU?!"

"OMG! Am I late?"

"Time change. Duh. Next flight?"

Dad would not be pleased that I had to pay penalty to switch flights. I'd need to come up with a good cover story.

The line to the ticket counter was a dozen people deep. It moved as slow as a stretch mark.

"I saw your little friends tromp through the concourse awhile ago," the clerk said, swiping my card. "TSA won't be amused. They didn't think it was funny the first time."

Every eye was on me as I approached the security line. A lumpy woman check-marked my ticket and waved me through, refusing to even speak. I kicked my heels off, adding them to the grey tub that already held my purse.

"Cold?" the pudgy man asked, waving me through the metal detector.

"Not particularly," I said, padding through the scanner, which didn't peep.

"Can you step over here, ma'am?"

"Why? It didn't beep."

"Just step over here, ma'am," the man insisted, probably a perv. I was probably the most action he had gotten since high school.

They made me stand on display until the next available woman was free. She donned rubber gloves and proceeded to pat me down, concentrating on my breasts and crotch.

"Satisfied?" I asked, frost in my voice.

"I don't know what you girls were thinking," she said, motioning to my negligee. "If you dress like this, we have to check you manually. And then we have to report unusual activity which means we have to manually check everyone until my boss gives us the okay."

"So?" I said, gathering my purse and heels.

"Contrary to belief, we don't enjoy this," she said, tossing away the gloves and squirting antibacterial gel on her hands.

"Yeah, right," I said, strutting off, the crowd's eyes probably caressing my silk covered backside.

During the two hours of sitting in the boarding area, three men offered me a coat, a crone offered me her afghan, and a baby mama offered me her hooter hider. I had clothes in my carryon but I'd be damned if I was going to slink off to cover up. Let them enjoy the view.

"I'm fine," I repeated after each offer, never looking up from my furious texting to my sorority sisters. Bree swore they called my room and Roxie had knocked.

"We thought you were already there."

Yeah right, I thought.

When my section was called, I stood and stretched, which raised the flimsy material of my baby doll top past my pierced navel. I felt all eyes snap to me.

"Have a good flight," the dowdy stewardess said, beeping my bar code, never looking at me.

I strutted down the gangplank like it was a catwalk. As I entered the airplane cabin, once again, I felt every eye on me.

"Scuse me," I purred, slithering past a sweating business man who was wrestling with his brief case. I sashayed down the aisle until I reached 15C, the window seat.

"Hello," said my seat mate, beaming up at me. Her face looked like boiled brains.

"Hello."

I slid past her to the window seat, trying not to stare. She was wearing a lavender top but shiny, mottled skin ran up her neck before transforming into angry red swirls. She wore flesh colored elbow length gloves.

"Well, you've been a lifesaver," she said, pleasantly as I settled in.

"Scuse me?" I said, avoiding her lashless, unblinking eyes.

"As soon as I saw you, I suddenly understood why no one was looking at me." She grimaced at me, which I guessed was a smile. Her crimson lips were livid and overstuffed. "So thank you."

"For what?" I said, inching away.

"Do you know how long it has been since I have

ventured out in public and not been stared at?" She smiled again, patting my hand. "I might need to take a half naked co-ed with me every time I go out in public."

She chuckled, a gargling sound.

"How do you do it?" I asked. She seemed nice. I wondered what she looked like before.

"Same as you, I imagine," she said, leaning back, straining the fragile web of skin on her neck. "I know everyone will stare and I do my best to ignore it."

I stared, now that her eyes were closed. Her glossy skin crumpled into a deep wince.

"Are you okay?"

She nodded.

"I'm okay," she said, finally. "It was rough going through security. They tried to be gentle but it hurts to be touched. I was hoping for the scanner."

"I'm sorry," I said, glad she wasn't looking at me.

"It's not your fault. Or theirs. They're just doing their job." She took a steadying breath and trained her unflinching eyes on mine.

"I'm sure the search was just as painful for them and as it was for me. But I bet you sure made their day."

I had no words. A molten lump of guilt sat in my stomach and for the first time that day, I was cold.

"Beauty and the beast," she said, quietly, resting her eyes again. She patted my hand once more, causing us both pain.

7

SIGHT UNSEEN

NOTHING IN LIFE REMAINED WORTH SEEING but that didn't mean Nessa wanted to go blind.

Widowed and alone, life had seemed dim before, but nothing prepared her for the sudden blackness which shuttered her vision in a single moment. Now, months later, a brush of the cat's tail threw her into a clawing panic. Creeping sensations inched along her skin until she batted them away. Once she smacked away a sunbeam which fell on her neck like a sultry breath.

Her son dutifully chaperoned her to doctor's offices and clinics, each with their metallic scents and probing fingers but her vision remained black.

"My company's conducting a clinical trial specifically for blindness," Lind said one day. Named after his father, he only used his middle name. Other than their business acumen, the men shared little else. "It's simply eye drops. It can't hurt to try."

She was surprised he had taken her condition to heart. Nessa agreed, tears leaking. Fear was so wearying. Nothing could be worse than this darkness.

The drive was disorienting and the echoing hallway frightened her. Random voices greeted her CEO son, their tone reverent. Finally, a gentle doctor reclined her chair and dribbled stinging drops into her eyes. Nessa blinked furiously. Rivulets ran down the wrinkled canals of her crow's feet and dampened her temples. Her seat rose and she gripped the arm rest.

"How do you feel?" Lind asked.

Nessa blinked, focused on the ever-present black. In amazement, each blink added new clarity, a Polaroid developing with a blink rather than a shake.

"What do you see?" Lind asked. His face floated into view. His brow was knotted with concern but she could make out his overgrown ears and receding hairline.

"I can see you," she said, tears blurring the vision. She brushed them away, not wanting to miss one sight.

"Amazing," he said. "I'd never guess you'd react this quickly."

The doctor peered into her miracle eyes and breathed bologna sandwich into her face.

"Fascinating," he said. "Total recovery. Let's check your vision, shall we? See if you need reading glasses maybe."

Nessa chuckled, considering the last book she read was at Blake's bedside over ten years ago. After Blake's death, it hadn't seem worth the trouble to read. And then there wasn't the possibility.

When the lights went dark in the room, a large letter E was illuminated on the far wall. Ambient light illuminated a profile of a man standing in the corner. It was Blake and he shook with rage and grief. His hair was tousled, his glasses oversized. He looked like he did in the early 70s, his quaking legs clad in blue bell bottoms.

"Blake?"

"Yes, Mother?" Her son answered, behind her.

"Not you. Your father! He's right there," she said. She tried to motion to the corner but her arms held a bundle. In a glance she knew it was Isadora, her blue baby girl, born without breath or heartbeat. Nessa cried out, marveling at the aching weight in her arms.

"Mother, are you okay?" Lind asked. He flipped the light on and dissolved her two lost loves, like sugar in water.

"Turn it off! Turn it off!" Nessa screamed. When Lind reluctantly clicked off the lights, her arms and the corner remained empty. They were gone. Nessa sobbed.

On the way home, she marveled at the verdant green leaves against the dying sherbet sky.

"I must have imagined it," she offered.

Lind remained skeptical but he eventually left her to her dusty, sparse home.

Her electricity bill would hit the stratosphere but she didn't care. She could see again. Nevertheless, before bed, Nessa strolled through her home switching them off with reluctance.

She resisted sleep, the smothering darkness. She tried reading a left behind book, but the wordy descriptions were pale shadows of the sights she'd rather see. Switching off the bedside light, she concentrated on her windup clock as it ticked away the night. Then she heard serrated breathing on the vacant pillow, next to her head.

"Who's there?"

Startled upright, she instantly recognized Blake, pale in the dark. He sucked in breath, just as he had when she called the ambulance. It frightened her then, as it did now. There was desperation in the sucking of air, his eyes frenetic.

"Blake! Sweetheart, it's me. I'm right here," she leaned over his struggling form. He shuddered under her hands.

"Ness…call…911," his voice echoed from the past.

"I'll call," she said, turning to flip on the light. Caught in the moment's web, it seemed perfectly rational to call an ambulance for a ghost, already dead a decade.

Light covered the room and when Nessa turned to the bed, the sheets were empty, the room silent.

"Blake?"

Nessa struggled out of the bed and approached the shadowy hall. Embracing the darkness, she called for her dead husband.

But it wasn't Blake who stood at the hall entrance. It was her mother, still in her apron and severe bun.

"Mother?"

The woman leveled a stern glare, transporting Nessa to her childhood. Mother held their thick, wooden spoon in her callused hand and Nessa remembered the vicious blows on her tender thighs.

The hallway light banished her, the wooden spoon clunking to the hardwood floor. Nessa couldn't bring herself to retrieve it.

From the dark living room, a warm glow beckoned her to the kitchen.

"Blake?"

Hellish flames greeted her. Flickering tongues licked the Harvest Gold cabinets, blackening them. A wave of heat singed nostril hairs and reignited the scars on her hands. Once again, the lights doused the flames, returning her kitchen to its bland ecru of today.

She abandoned her search for Blake and fell asleep sprawled in his recliner, the room ablaze with incandescent light.

Nessa cringed away from the drops the next morning. She shared her visions from the night before. She wished she couldn't see Lind's doubt.

"I'm sure it was just a bad dream," he said.

Nessa led him to the hall, where her mother's spoon had been. But it was gone.

"Okay, no drops today. But I'm going to talk to your doctor about getting some anti-anxiety medication."

Sighted and wary, Nessa's day crept by. Dozing after the fitful night, she didn't notice the dying light until the burglar from 1999 smashed the glass door. As he slid his gloved hand through the jagged glass, Nessa dove for the side lamp.

Where were her pleasant memories, the moments she wanted to relive? Why couldn't she hold Blake's hand, instead of witnessing his death? Why couldn't she tousle Lind's head once more, instead of watching a dresser fall on him, crushing his tiny arm?

Haunted and horrific memories crept out of low-lit shadows over the long week.

Even with the lights burning, she could feel the movements around her. She heard the bat fly out of the chimney flue. In the moments between quick blinks, she felt its powder wings brush her hair.

"I wish I had never taken those drops. I should just pluck out my eyes."

She had thought about it. Gouging out the offending orbs couldn't be as painful as childbirth. Then her special brand of hell would be over.

"Mother," Lind said, hesitating. "I'm worried for you. I didn't want to share this but you were given placebo drops. It was nothing but saline. I suspected your blindness was hysterical and then you were better. Your visions aren't real."

Impossible.

Her son had lied to her. And her body had betrayed her. Hysterical blindness and now faux visions? Reeling, her vision wavered.

"Mother, I think you should move someplace safer. This house holds too many bad memories. Maybe an apartment at Sunscape?"

She remained mute, processing the betrayal, his and hers. How could she protect herself from an enemy with outposts in her head?

As Lind opened the door to leave, he scanned the bruised horizon.

"It looks like a storm is coming, Mother. Shall I fetch your flashlight?"

He had to go. He had a family waiting for him at home. His wife resented his constant absences. Nessa understood. She had been a wife once, too, with an ailing mother-in-law.

Nessa lit every candle, creating a pyre on her coffee table. Pockets crammed with flashlights, she held two like billy-clubs.

Lightning flashed, a disco light for her demons. A crashing boom preceded the snuffing out of all the power. Nessa sat, flashlights looping the room like search lights. Her young brother, Lucas, stood in front of her, a wicked smile on his freckled face.

"Nessy, guess what I got?"

Nessa shook her head, refusing to answer. He gleefully held out a sealed Mason jar. She knew what was inside: a black widow spider. Lucas would dangle it inches from her face, on a stick.

She squeezed her eyes shut. Lucas spun open the jar.

What you can't see, can't hurt you. It's not real, Nessa told herself. But tears leaked from her eyes as Lucas taunted.

"Open your eyes, Nessy. Look at the pretty spider."

Decades ago, she had run screaming to her mother.

It's not real, she said. But Nessa felt the stick brush her hair. She felt the spider creep across her cheek and onto her eyelid.

Don't touch it! It's not real!

She trembled in terror. Lightning flashed blood red through her closed lids, illuminating the thick spider. The light could only offer her reprieve, never relief.

"Nessy," Lucas taunted, twirling the stick in her hair, tickling the spider from its perch. She felt it creep down her neck. "Come join us, Nessy."

And between strobes of light, the spider bites.

8

GINGERBREAD

MY GINGERBREAD BUNDT CAKE sold for eleven dollars at the craft bazaar auction. Hard to believe but that's the God's honest truth. I've been making that cake for thirty odd years and my family just scarfs it down. But no one gets worked up about it. It is just one of those things we eat at Christmas. Well, except for this year.

I get butterflies just thinking about tonight. I don't think a momma should be afraid of her kids but my three are as alien to me as those dark babies the Girtz's keep adopting. Now with Leroy dead and cold in the ground for five months, I just don't know how Christmas is gonna play out.

God bless him but Leroy was just as much of a problem as the children. Mixed together, like the Molotov cocktails Leroy would throw on the campfires, they would explode when put in close proximity and triggered. Now that he ain't here, drunk, I should be breathing easy. But my kids scare me all on their own.

Darlene is smart as a whip, top of her class in school

along with being voted Homecoming Queen. She has a right pretty house in town and a silent husband. As the oldest and the bossiest, she is a force to be reckoned with.

Philip on the other hand seems to have no force at all. He walks around, like the wind got knocked out of him, letting life buffet him around like a piece of driftwood. Handsome and smart too, he don't seem to know how to pick hisself up. And ain't nothing too terrible happen to him yet neither!

Colleen took all the ugly things from her Daddy and me and made them beautiful. My bushy eyebrows which look like wandering caterpillars. Well; she inherited them and tamed them to her eyes, looking like pagodas. Leroy's angry Lake Michigan eyes are sunny blue skies on her. She just don't understand people.

I don't care much that I am ugly but I regret being dumb. Being ugly and dim, that's the cross God gave me to bear. My place was in the home, being Leroy's wife, which I knew was a gift of God. I could have never married on my own. It was all God's doing. And who am I to argue if He used liquor to get it done.

When Leroy got diagnosed with lung cancer, it was too far advanced to even do anything. At first he only got a little weaker but still smoked several packs a day. But as the cancer grew in his lungs, it was like it ate up all his nastiness first. We had been married 29 years and he never once said 'I love you' to me. Sure, it bothered me at first, but I got used to it. He supported all of us and never raised a hand. 'Course, he'd get drunk regularly but never on benders like my no-good daddy.

When his cancer got so bad that he wasn't getting out of bed, he became a whole new person. The disgust in his eyes which had been there for all them years was gone. As I sat by his bedside, helping him play Solitaire, he looked at me when he talked. And he talked! Lordy Hallelujah! Instead of yelling or criticizing some stupid thing I did, he talked to me. We'd watch the news and he'd comment on the new president, Ronnie, and how he got shot. And sometimes he'd even ask what I thought. My brain was rusty like our rototiller in the spring but with some use, we was having real conversations!

A few weeks before Leroy died, we was talking about the house and whether the roof needed to be replaced. Leroy, of course, couldn't do it but Philip was gonna put on a new one on come fall.

"I'd sure like it if they could leave some nails sticking out at the rafters so I can just string up the Christmas lights without much trouble," I suggested.

"Bernice," he said, "You are brilliant. That'd be right smart. Remember to tell Philip that when we see 'im."

I didn't know which was better, being called Bernice or being told I was smart. I felt as light as my momma's angel food cake.

And now it's our first Christmas Eve without Leroy. I had to fight Darlene to have it back here. It wasn't her fault that last year went so badly. Every year goes badly. Well, it might be a little her fault. She just don't know how to accept things as they are. She is always trying to force the world to go her way. I'm always telling her the "Let go and let God" but she don't know how to get out of God's way.

Besides the lack of gingerbread, dinner was the same dishes we always have: sugared ham, mashed potatoes with lumps, green bean casserole, Harvard beets, Parker house rolls, and cranberry jelly from the can. And only pie for dessert.

It shouldn't feel no different. Leroy was never there for the getting ready part anyway. He was usually down at the bar until at least six. Colleen worked the breakfast and lunch shift today and ain't back yet. Philip's closing up the shop at five o'clock, he said. Darlene and Kurt would show up at their usual time with her "Hi-de-ho" at the door.

Even though the house is exactly as it has been every other year, it feels quieter. I peek into Colleen's room and unplug her clock radio. I set it on the kitchen window ledge, moving several onion roots to the counter. Plugged in, Colleen's music comes blaring out! Startled, I nearly knock it in the soap suds. I spin the dial to the left, looking for something I recognized.

"I'll be home for Christmas
You can count on me
Please have snow and mistletoe
And presents under the tree…"

Bing Crosby croons in my kitchen and I sing along. I stir up the Harvard beets, keeping time with the music. The cuckoo clock chimes five o'clock and I took a little twirl, feeling light on my feet. On my last turn, I catch a glimpse of Darlene's furious face in the silver stock pot.

***

"A toast," Philip proposes, holding up a Flintstone jelly jar full of Black Velvet he dug out of my freezer.

"This is ridiculous," Darlene mutters. "I'm not drinking it."

"Fine. The rest of us will. A toast," he continues. "To Dad, may he rest in peace."

"Amen," I said.

Kurt, Philip, Colleen and I all clink our glasses. Philip's is significantly fuller than ours but we all sip.

"It's not that I don't want to honor Dad," Darlene started. "It's just that I might be pregnant and I don't want to take the chance."

"You pregnant again?" Colleen asked, uninterested.

"That's the thing. I don't know if I am pregnant which is why I can't take a drink, in case I am. I saw Dr. Combs again this week," she restarted eagerly.

"Good for you. Did you see the doctor yet, Mom?" Philip interrupted. We had all had enough of Darlene's pregnancy talk.

"Yes, he said everything was fine." I finished simply, hoping to have set an example for Darlene. No one was actually interested in your health problems; they just asked to be polite.

Christmas had already started off wrong. Darlene was horrified to find me dancing in the kitchen.

"You're dancing on his grave!" she shrieked, flapping her arm like her coat pockets were on fire.

"No, I am not. I'm dancing in the kitchen."

"You would never have danced if Daddy was here."

"No, probably not," I admitted. I might as well plead guilty.

"So you're happy Daddy is gone!"

"No. It's just a different time. I was in the Christmas spirit."

Colleen entered the hullabaloo to accuse me of stealing her radio.

"I didn't steal it. It's right here."

"But you went into my room!"

"You are the only one who has a radio."

"That's because I am the only one who listens to one. Why are you listening to one?"

"She was dancing," Darlene said, scandalized.

"So?"

"Daddy just died!" Darlene spat as she spoke.

"Five months ago," Colleen said reasonably and left the room.

Darlene made a half hearted attempt to get Kurt riled up but mostly she marked her time until Philip came home, attacking him immediately with my scandal.

"Mom was dancing!" Darlene announced, before Philip

had even shut the front door.

"With who?" he asked, perplexed.

"No one. She was just dancing in the kitchen by herself. With Daddy dead and all."

"So? Dad's dead whether she dances or not."

Thank you, Philip, I thought. All of Darlene's steam was redirected when Philip suggested toasting Leroy with a shot of Black Velvet.

"That's just tacky," she objected.

"Why?" Philip asked.

"We should do something classier, like lighting a candle or planting a tree," she offered.

"We should plant a tree in the middle winter in Michigan?" Philip asked, pouring a second shot.

"And when have you ever seen Daddy light a candle?" Colleen asked.

"A cigarette, maybe," I offered, smiling.

"There ya go, Dar. We'll light up a cigarette every December to honor Dad," said Philip.

"You are all just crass," Darlene spat, stomping from the room.

Crass or not, we all drank to Leroy. And thirty years after I married Leroy, the first taste of alcohol passed my lips. It burned at the lump in my throat and gave an excuse for the tears in my eyes.

"Dinner will be ready in about 15 minutes," I said, gathering up the glasses and escaping to the kitchen.

I peeked in the oven and then turned off the potatoes.

"What can I do to help, Mom?" Darlene asked, sneaking in.

"Why don't you fill the celery sticks?"

"Why bother? No one eats them," she said, opening the fridge.

The silence weighed heavily and I clinked the pans to fill the space.

"Mom?"

"Yeah?"

"You know what I don't like?"

"What?"

"Lumps in my potatoes," she said with a mischievous grin.

"You know, I'd have to agree."

"Let's take a vote." And she disappeared into the living room, reappearing a minute later with a triumphant grin.

"We all like creamy mashed potatoes. Is that doable?"

"I can do that," I said, mashing with renewed vigor. I wondered where they tasted creamy mashed potatoes.

***

Later, seated around the groaning table with the Leroy's spot as empty as Jesus' tomb, we side stepped landmines as we passed dishes. Traditionally dinner was round one of bickering.

"Dig in!" I announced.

"You've outdone yourself, Mom," Philip said as he ladled gravy.

"It looks wonderful," Darlene agreed.

As we chewed, swallowed and sipped, we discussed the weather, the cost of brake fluid and Colleen's biggest tip ($12) from a man dressed like Santa. We looked and sounded like a normal family but we were cautiously skirting any suspicious lumps.

"Remember how Dad always made a volcano out of his food?" Colleen asked, kicking a landmine solidly. The clattering abruptly stopped.

"Yeah, that was pretty disgusting," Darlene admitted, smiling at Colleen.

"He said it was all going to the same place," Philip reminded us.

"I don't know how he managed to eat it," I said.

"I loved the way he could make the cards arch when he

shuffled them," Darlene whispered, the small gem presented as an offering.

"Remember when Dad shot that four point buck from the pick up truck window, as we drove like maniac across the corn field?!" Philip threw his offering on the pile.

"He could whistle a tune he had only heard one time," Kurt said.

Everyone looked to me. I paused.

"Your daddy loved gingerbread," I offered in reverence.

***

It was the last Saturday Leroy lived to see. He had been steadily losing weight and strength. His breath came in rattled gasps. The home nurse said any day now.

Saturday morning had arrived with a vengeance, its rude bright light invading the living room. I had pulled the drapes shut blocking some of the insistent sunshine.

Leroy weakly motioned me with his fingers.

"I want gingerbread," he whispered hoarsely.

"Gingerbread?"

"Yes."

"It's July," I argued.

"Yes, but I won't be here for Christmas."

These were the statements that broke my heart.

"Okay sweetie. I will make you some gingerbread," I patted his hand, affectionately. He squeezed my fingers back, surprising me.

"Now," he said, insistent yet diminished.

"Okay." I rushed to the kitchen and made my bundt cake, fearing my time away from him. My whisk was a blur in the bowl and the second the pan hit the oven rack, I was back by his side.

The ginger scent enveloped the room.

His eyes were closed and I studied his chest for movement. A gurgled rattle escaped his lips as he slowly opened his eyes and looked at me for an eternity.

"Tell me about heaven," he whispered.

"What do you mean?"

"Tell me about your God in heaven," he breathed in then out. "Is he real?"

"Oh, yes."

"How do you know?"

"I just believe. I have seen his hand at work in my life ever since I met him."

"But how do I find him?"

"Stand still and ask him to find you." I could barely breathe for the pressure in my chest.

"What if he doesn't want to find me?" Leroy's blue eyes turned watery. I had never him cry. Ever.

"Oh, honey,." I breathed, clasping his hands. "Then he wouldn't have come looking for you. He has been right here all along."

"And it's not too late for me?" he asked, his voice a little boy's whisper.

"No. It's not too late. You just have to tell him you need his help."

Just then the buzzer rang. I stifled a curse.

"Be right back." I rushed to the kitchen and yanking out the gingerbread cake. I cut a slice immediately, burning my fingers and rushed with the plate back to Leroy's side.

He was sleeping again and I held his hand for long minutes. Finally he opened them again and smiled.

"I have your gingerbread cake for you," I offered. He hadn't eaten food in days and could barely keep down ice chips. But I would do whatever he asked. He moved to lift his head and I quickly stood to help. I tucked a pillow under his head, smoothed his sheets and cut off a small bite.

"Here you go," I said, gently easing the fork to his cracked lips.

One morsel entered his mouth and he closed his eyes.

"How is it?" I asked.

"Just like heaven," he answered, closing his eyes in eternal rest.

9

DEATH IN TANDEM

DEATH IS ALL AROUND if we only look.

Nations of ants die in our yards, cannibalized by cousin bugs or bully birds. Possum, coons, and the neighbor's hunting dogs get flattened, life slipping away as their once warm bodies become a cold speed bump. Eventually the county comes and scrapes them off the asphalt, carting away the stench and reminder.

Death is everywhere and Mason's eyes were trained to see it. Jenny's death had peeled back the soft fur, leaving only the slimy entrails of death and its contamination.

The ambulance got lost coming for her, but after futile attempts and pointless prayers, she was eventually planted in the ground and labeled, just like her tidy garden.

"Will another Aunt Jenny grow there?" her niece had asked and Mason understood her point. Why label a patch of ground if you don't expect a crop?

Now Jenny's garden was two years overgrown, indistinguishable from the brambles behind it. At the shed,

Mason strung up butchered rabbits like so much summer laundry. Fifteen bucks already hung on the clothes line, painting the grass below bright red. He had just snapped another neck and slid the knife under the dewlap when he heard the whine.

Overhead, a black smoke trail chased a small plane across the sky, trailing down. The small plane shrieked as it spun twice and then bottomed out to a steep decline.

Mason held the white rabbit motionless in mid-air, watching the plane pinwheel towards the ground. The plane disappeared behind the tree line and he waited.

He heard no noise and felt no impact. But a moment later a thin stream of black smoke rose above the spot.

He drove quickly towards Phoenix Lake, misdialing 911, keeping the smoke plume in sight and dialing again. The plane was tucked in a wooded lot near a hunting trail. It sat propped up against a sturdy tree, like a walking stick. Dirty smoke climbed out of the turbines while fluids leaked out of the bottom. The alcove reeked of jet fuel and turned earth.

"Hello?" he called out to the plane's carcass, knowing better than to expect an answer.

A tiny sound echoed in the silence. At first, he thought it was the moan of a tree leaning in the wind but then he heard it again.

"Hello?"

"Help," a woman's voice called from inside the wreckage. Mason stood rooted to the spot, unbelieving. She called out a second time and he was spurred to movement.

"Hang on! I'm coming!"

Laddering up a wing, he couldn't reach the side door above him. The pilot's window was splattered red and spider-webbed with cracks. Mason dropped down and angled his head in, trying to see around the dead pilot.

"Are you there?" she asked from the shadows. Mason counted three men with bloodied faces and blank expressions. She was hidden behind a bulkhead but he calculated her location in the dim interior.

"Don't move," Mason cautioned. "Help is on the way."

There was no answer from within the plane and his hope sputtered.

"Hey! Stay with me. What's your name?"

"Jennifer," was the soft answer. The plane shifted with an audible creak.

"Whadayaknow, my wife's name was Jennifer, Jenny actually."

"Was?"

"She died."

The mistake of his words echoed across the empty chamber.

"Are the men okay?" she asked, shifting and then groaning. "We're going to a conference. I just met them."

He didn't answer. Weren't there professionals for this kind of news? He thought of the dead rabbits hoisted like surrender flags three miles away. He looked at the blood that watered the earth below. And finally with reluctance, he thought of his Jenny's blood being washed away by the coroner.

"You're gonna be fine," Mason said, willing the words to be true.

In the distance, he heard the winding up of sirens. He smiled at her through the dim light, letting her know the experts were on their way. The emergency workers swarmed the area, skinning the wounded plane and dismantling it liked a dressed rabbit. Jennifer crawled out herself, standing and wincing but alive.

"Hey you," she said, smiling weakly.

"Hey back," he answered.

They shared an awkward handshake, wobbling towards a hug and then away. He patted her shoulder before they whisked her off to the ambulance and away.

"You two know each other?" an officer asked.

"Nope, just met."

"She's lucky to be alive," he said. A platitude.

"Aren't we all?"

It was then Mason noticed the other sounds around him.

Bird song.

Bug chatter.

Heron call.

Frog croak.

Snake slither.

The woods were teeming with life. It was all around, if only we looked.

ABOUT THE AUTHOR

Nicole Amsler is 50% novelist, 45% sarcastic, 30% book club fanatic, 15% copywriter, 10% caffeinated, and bad at math.
She is also a wife to Mark and Momma to Delaney and Spencer, as well as the designated kitty litter scooper, garden overseer, and the only person who knows were anything is.

Please visit my website at www.nicoleamsler.com for book club resources, upcoming books and stories, recipes, and for woefully sporadic thoughts. I can also be found on Facebook, Twitter, and Pinterest.

Made in the USA
Charleston, SC
20 May 2013